NEW1

Newton's Brain

A Romanetto

BY JAKUB ARBES

Translated from the Czech by David Short

JANTAR PUBLISHING

London 2023

First published in London, Great Britain in 2023 by
Jantar Publishing Ltd
www.jantarpublishing.com

First Czech edition was published,
as *Newtonův mozek*,
in Prague, in 1877

HISTORICAL SCIENCE FICTION LIBRARY
Book I

NEWTON'S BRIAN
Jakub Arbes

Translation © David Short 2023
The right of David Short to be identified as translator of this work has been
asserted in accordance with the Copyright, Design and Patents Act 1988.

Introduction © Peter Zusi
Afterword © David Short

Cover and book design © Davor Pukljak, Frontispis.hr
All illustrations made with the help of Midjourney AI

A CIP record of this book is available from the British Library
ISBN 978–1–914990–21–2

Printed and bound on paper sourced from sustainable forests by
Imprint Digital, Exeter, England

This translation was made possible by a grant from the
Ministry of Culture of the Czech Republic

MINISTRY OF CULTURE
CZECH REPUBLIC

Contents

Time Mastered, Time Shattered:
Jakub Arbes and the Literary Time Machine
by Peter Zusi (University College London)

There is a peculiar intrigue in discovering that a familiar scientific concept or literary theme has an older, more unusual, provenance than is generally supposed. Certain properties of modern quantum physics, for example, have surprising correlates in Presocratic philosophy and in ancient Vedic texts; and many of the tales famous from Chaucer's *Canterbury Tales* and Boccaccio's *Decameron* have their origin in far older Arabic and Persian literary sources. When we turn to the modern literary genre of Science Fiction, one of the canonical motifs is that of a machine allowing travel forwards and backwards through time: temporal movement analogous to the spatial liberation made possible by technological revolutions in modern transportation, from the railroad in the nineteenth century to the airplane and space rocket in the twentieth. The literary origin of this motif of the time machine is commonly associated with H. G. Wells's famous work, *The Time Machine: An Invention*. Published in 1895, this was Wells's first published novel, though it developed themes he had been thinking about since his story 'The Chronic Argonauts', published in a student magazine in 1888. *The Time Machine* has been called 'the foundational text of modern Science Fiction,'[1] and the subtitle 'An Invention' might

---

1   Fredric Jameson, *Archaeologies of the Future: The Desire Called Utopia and Other Science Fictions* (London: Verso, 2005), p. 99. Jameson's claim competes with another, at least equally plausible identification of Mary Shelley's *Frankenstein, Or, The Modern Prometheus* (1818) as the foundational text of science fiction; see, e.g., Paul K. Alkon, *Science Fiction Before 1900: Imagination Discovers Technology* (New York and London: Routledge, 2002), p. 1. Shelley's *Frankenstein*, of course, does not engage with the notion of time travel.

be taken to refer not only to the time machine invented by Wells's nameless Time Traveller, but also to Wells's own invention of the time machine as literary device. Such notions of foundation and invention undergird the often unquestioning identification of Wells as the inventor of the time machine in literature.[2]

This makes it all the more intriguing to find a literary depiction of a time machine in a little-known work of Czech literature from 1877: the present novella by Jakub Arbes (1840–1914), bearing the striking title *Newton's Brain*.

The notion of a time machine appears to have emerged gradually in literature, and while Arbes's overlooked novella may not be the very first literary depiction (I leave such judgments to historians of Science Fiction) it is certainly among the earliest. [3] One of the reasons the emergence of this literary motif was gradual is that literary depictions of a time *machine* were long preceded by literary depictions of time *travel*. [4] The latter theme is venerable, and in many respects would appear a natural creation of human consciousness: our ability to remember past events or to imagine possible (often utopian)

2   Charles M. Tung describes Wells's *The Time Machine* as 'the first appearance of such a device'; Charles M. Tung, *Modernism and Time Machines* (Edinburgh: Edinburgh University Press, 2019) p. 1. Alkon writes: 'In *The Time Machine*, explanations of the time machine itself may be dismissed as scientific patter at its most obfuscating: such devices are impossible. As a literary convention initiated by Wells and indispensable to later science fiction, however, the time machine deserves high praise' (Alkon, *Science Fiction Before 1900*, p. 49).

3   I am unaware of any English-language account of time-travel or time-machine fiction that mentions Arbes.

4   David Wittenberg offers what he calls a 'more dialectical, and messier' account of the origins of time travel fiction, in which Wells is only one among several important figures, but he does not distinguish systematically between time travel and time machines; David Wittenberg, *Time Travel: The Popular Philosophy of Narrative* (New York: Fordham University Press, 2013), p. 44.

futures is, in an important sense, a form of time travel; and writing, literary writing in particular, is inherently a journey through time in that it gives expression to and brings alive moments that either no longer or do not yet exist, representing presents that are not our own.[5] Eighteenth- and especially nineteenth-century literature were particularly rich in time-travel narratives, most of which would not fit under even a capacious understanding of Science Fiction. These narratives often utilized supernatural narrative devices such as hauntings and ghosts (Charles Dickens's *A Christmas Carol*, 1843) or unnaturally extended sleep (Louis-Sébastien Mercier's *L'An 2440, rêve s'il en fut jamais*, 1771; Washington Irving's 'Rip Van Winkle', 1819; Edward Bellamy's *Looking Backward 2000–1887*, 1888). Occasionally time travel was depicted as a product of intoxication ('Rip Van Winkle' again; or the 1888 satirical novel by the Czech author Svatopluk Čech, *The New, Epoch-Making Excursion by Mr. Brouček, This Time to the 15th Century*). And occasionally narratives would present time travel without any attempt to provide an explanation (Mark Twain's 'A Connecticut Yankee in King Arthur's Court', 1889), or simply imagined the distant future without any account of time travel as such (Vladimir Odoevsky's *The Year 4338: Petersburg letters*, 1835). A time *machine* narrative, by contrast, foregoes such supernatural or satirical premises and connects the idea of time travel with the distinctly modern themes of technology, science, and rationality. So unsurprisingly, the

---

5   As Wittenberg writes, 'since even the most elementary narratives, whether fictional or nonfictional, set out to modify or manipulate the order, duration, and significance of events in time – that is, since all narratives do something like "travel" through time or construct "alternate" worlds – one could arguably call narrative itself a "time machine"'; ibid., p. 9.

concepts that would allow such connection and would shape early time machines in literature emerged first in scientific speculation and in the nascent popular science writing of the nineteenth century.

In fact, the source for Arbes's conception of his time machine can be pinpointed quite precisely, though this has not, as far as I am aware, been noticed in the existing secondary literature. In 1846 a small pamphlet was published anonymously in London with the title *The Stars and the Earth; Or, Thoughts Upon Space, Time, and Eternity*.[6] This small book, revealed in later editions as the work of the Berlin-born lawyer, author and amateur astronomer Felix Eberty (1812–1884), became a publishing sensation when it appeared and it continued to be influential into the twentieth century.[7] A prominent scholar of Franz Kafka has speculated that the pamphlet influenced not only Kafka's writing but Albert Einstein's special theory of

---

6   Anonymous, *The Stars and the Earth; Or, Thoughts Upon Space, Time, and Eternity* (London: H. Bailliere, 1846).

7   Eberty now seems to be as absent from English-language scholarship on time-travel literature as is Arbes. But a second volume of *The Stars and the Earth* appeared in 1847 and opened with extracts from rapturous reviews of volume one. *The Border Watch* wrote: 'Our readers, we are confident, will thank us for introducing them to "The Stars and the Earth". Perhaps nothing we have ever read, of uninspired man's penmanship, has excited within us, sensations of a more startling, yet pleasurable kind.' The *Family Herald* wrote: 'This little book contains a new idea, which is saying a great deal in these times of intelligence, when all creation is ransacked by the genii of poetry, philosophy, science, and theology, for something new, striking, and entertaining. It is an idea, too, which is infinitely sublime and beautiful. It is one of the most poetical ideas which the human mind can entertain – an idea which is not merely chimerical and imaginary, but based on scientific facts, and logically true. We wonder it has never been hit upon before.' *The Critic* wrote: 'Forty-eight small pages, suggesting food for a life of thought.' *The Stars and the Earth; Or, Thoughts Upon Space, Time, and Eternity*, Part II (London: H. Bailliere, 1847), pp. 11–12.

relativity as well. [8] Kafka's familiarity with the work can only be conjectured, though it seems plausible; Einstein's familiarity is documented, as he wrote an introduction to a new edition of the work in 1923. Arbes's familiarity is also supposition, but given the at times extraordinarily exact echoes of *The Stars and the Earth* in *Newton's Brain*, the supposition seems safe.

Eberty starts with an observation that by the 1840s was already widely known even to a lay public: though light travels at a speed that to the human eye seems instantaneous, to traverse the enormous distances involved over cosmic space light requires measurable time. He writes: 'We do not see the sun as it now is, but as it was eight minutes before; Jupiter as it was fifty-two minutes; Uranus as it was more than two hours before; the star in Centaur as it was three years ago; Vega as it was nine and a quarter years; and a star of the 12th magnitude as it was four thousand years ago'. [9] (Arbes repeats these reference points nearly verbatim.) Though the notion that to look into the night sky was *de facto* to look into the past was not new, Eberty's original twist was to imagine the reversed perspective as well: that the past of the Earth, all of human history, was somewhere 'out there' in the night sky as well. He writes:

8   See Hans-Gerd Koch, 'Franz Kafka und die Veränderung der Wahrnehmung von Raum, Zeit und Bewegung', in *Kafka und Prag: Literatur-, kultur-, sozial-, und sprachhistorische Kontexte*, ed. by Peter Becher, Steffan Höhne, and Marek Nekula (Köln: Bölau, 2012), 265–73 (esp. pp. 269–70). A German-language edition of *The Stars and the Earth* appeared under the initials F.Y. in Breslau also in 1846 with the title *Die Gestirne und die Weltgeschichte; Gedanken über Zeit, Raum und Ewigkeit*. Koch describes the English-language edition as a pirated translation. Oddly, a later German-language edition from 1860 did not republish the original German but translated the English version back into German; see *Meyers Konversationslexikon*, 4th ed. (1885–1892), consulted online: *https://www.retrobibliothek.de/retrobib/seite.html?id=104680#Eberty* (accessed 3 September 2023).

9   *The Stars and the Earth*, [Part I], pp. 21–22.

'[A]n imaginary observer in the moon would not see earth as it was at the moment of observation, but as it was five quarters of a second before. An observer from the sun sees the earth as it was eight minutes before. From Uranus the time between reality and the perception by the eye being two hours and a half apart; if, for example, the summit of the Alps on a certain morning was illumined by the first rays of the sun at six o'clock, an observer in this planet, who was provided either with the requisite power of vision, or a sufficiently good telescope, would see this indication of the rising of the sun at half-past eight of our time. [...] An observer in Vega would see what happened with us twelve years ago, and so on, until an inhabitant of a star of the 12th magnitude, if we imagine him with unlimited power of vision contemplating the earth, sees it as it was four thousand years ago, when Memphis was founded, and the Patriarch Abraham wandered upon its surface.

In the immeasurably great number of fixed stars which are scattered about in the universe, floating in æther at a distance of between fifteen and twenty billions of miles from us, reckoning backwards any given number of years, doubt-less a star could be found which sees the past epochs of our earth as if existing now [...].[10]

In this reversal of perspective lies the conceptual foundation Arbes drew upon for his own time machine in *Newton's Brain*.

Eberty also relies on the same two hypothetical instruments, to a modern reader quaintly absurd, as does Arbes: the ability

---

10   Ibid., pp. 23–25.

to move about the universe faster than light, and possession of 'a sufficiently good telescope' to be able to view details on earth across cosmic distances. (Arbes upgrades the telescope to spectacles, a sort of proto-Google goggles.) Eberty writes:

> [W]e may maintain that it is possible, i.e., not in contradiction to the laws of thought, that a man may travel to a star in a given time, and that he may effect this provided with so powerful a telescope as to be able to overcome every given distance, and every light and shadow in the object to be examined. With this supposition, and with the aid of a knowledge of the position and distance of every given fixed star […] it will be possible to recal [sic] sensibly to our very eyes, an actual and true representation of every moment of history that has passed. If, for instance, we wish to see Luther before the council at Worms, we must transport ourselves in a second to a fixed star, from which the light requires about three hundred years (or so much more or less), in order to reach the earth. Thence the earth will appear in the same state, and with the same persons moving upon it, as it actually was at the time of the Reformation.
>
> To the view of an observer from another fixed star, our Saviour appears now upon earth performing His miracles and ascending into Heaven; and thus every moment which has passed during the lapse of centuries down to the present time, may be actually recalled so as to be present. [11]

---

11   Ibid., pp. 35–36.

Modern readers must remind themselves that half a century before Einstein's special relativity the postulate of travelling faster than light was not as irrational as it sounds now. Further, Eberty emphasizes that his speculations revolve around theoretical *possibility*, not pragmatic *practicality*. Arbes works from the same premise and takes even more literary licence, imagining as he does such travel and vision being carried out in practice. But he too is more focused on exploring the principles involved than in claiming this travel to be plausible, so it would be misplaced for a modern reader to react with the sort of dismissiveness shown by the esteemed members of the assembly portrayed in *Newton's Brain*. (The same holds for other 'minor' details such as the need to breathe in outer space, to withstand the extraordinary forces of space travel, and so on.)

Eberty's reflections on cosmic principles provide Arbes with a further idea as well: that time is relative, its flow is fluid. Eberty imagines his observer on that star of the 12th magnitude travelling at such speed that he reaches our sun in an hour, all the while observing events on earth. He concludes that 'we have indubitably the following result: that before the eye of this observer the entire history of the world, from the time of Abraham to the present day, passes in the space of an hour'.[12] Arbes has his protagonist engage in similar speculation: 'anyone must concede that should one of us be able to make the roughly five-billion-mile trip from some star of magnitude 12 to here on Earth in an hour, with his sight artificially sharpened in the manner I have described, he would be able, in that brief time, to view scenes from the whole of human history

---

12   Ibid., pp. 40–41.

as we know it, from the first man down to this very moment...' (pp. 101–102). The notion that relative motion at great speeds would affect the passage of time – that time can be extended or compacted – has a distinctly twentieth-century ring.

Arbes's borrowings from Eberty thus embed this wildly imaginative novella in at least loosely scientific ground. Indeed in certain ways Arbes hews much more closely to a modern scientific attitude than does Eberty, who frames his reflections as a tool for greater understanding of divine omniscience and who is unable to conceive of a cosmic timescale beyond the Biblical framework. (Arbes, by contrast, grants to the universe an age of 30 million years. He pokes fun at the theologians in the assembly, who are quick to dismiss the beliefs of other religions as unfounded hypotheses but are dumbstruck at the suggestion that Christianity could be characterized in the same manner. He replaces the origin story of Adam and Eve in Eden with an episode of brute violence over basic means of subsistence.) Arbes's title itself, *Newton's Brain*, raises immediate expectations of a celebration of scientific discovery and of the progress of human reason. The phrase 'Newton's brain' sounds initially like synecdoche for scientific genius as such, but Arbes serves us a surprise: we get Newton's *brain* as a physical object, but not the rest of Newton. The phrase turns out to be neither synecdoche nor metaphor but refers literally to a prop of the plot. For the long-dead Newton's brain, nicked from a museum, has been unceremoniously deposited into another man's skull (that of the narrator's friend, allowing him to devise the ingenious instruments for his time travel).

This image of transplantation – hovering ambiguously between ancient, gruesome practices of trepanning and modern, miraculous surgeries – takes the depiction of science and rationality in *Newton's Brain* in unexpected directions. Most immediately, it connects the notion of human progress and the ideal of rationality with violence: the inventor states that he was only able to place Newton's brain inside his own brain cavity because his skull had been shattered open by the breech-loading rifles wielded by the Prussians in the 1866 Austro-Prussian war, rifles far superior technologically to the arms fielded by the Austrian army. At this point the inventor's narrative becomes a starkly pessimistic reflection on historical progress, noting that human ingenuity has done precious little to improve the fundamental state of human affairs. Once the scene of time travel itself takes place, it becomes nothing more than a litany of battles causing hideous, pointless loss of life – a litany whose monotony is surely intentional and hammers home the sheer brutality and waste of human history.

With this pessimism, bordering on nihilism, Arbes's *Newton's Brain* shares a significant trait with Wells's *Time Machine*. Wells depicts travel only into the future: a striking feature given that his fictional time machine is, unlike Arbes's, capable of travelling into both the future and the past. Wells's Time Traveller has eyes only for what progress the future of humanity will bring; and the initially intriguing scenario he encounters in the future becomes by stages increasingly gruesome and terrifying. His final scene, particularly chilling from the standpoint of the early 21st century, depicts an Earth utterly overcome by entropy, in the midst of fundamental climatic, geological and solar breakdown. Arbes casts his vision backwards and sees human history as ceaseless violent conflict. Why is it that these early fictions imagining the accomplishment of an age-old human wish – to be able to travel through time – have led to such dark, dystopian visions?

Readers will form their own answers to this question, but it is worth noting at least that the chronological structure underlying early literary conceptions of the time machine displays, as a matter of record, a stubborn connection to madness. While most of the best-known later depictions of time travel have favoured theoretical devices such as wormholes and similar forms of bending space-time (notions drawing loosely on post-Einsteinian physics) for the earliest literary time machines movement through time was predicated upon a chronologically uniform, linear model of time. From the eighteenth century on this model had increasingly challenged if not displaced traditional, chiliastic or theological models of time, which posit beginnings, narratives and endpoints that cannot be altered. But an open-ended, linear chronology – what the philosopher and critic Walter Benjamin referred to pejoratively in the late 1930s as 'homogeneous empty time' – is more easily understood as inviting movement of the imagination backwards and forwards along its scale. In this sense linear chronology might seem a force for clarity, rationality and stability: every point in time has a clear position on the timeline and an equal value. The problem, however, emerges with precisely the feature that distinguishes linear from theological chronological models: open-endedness. It may be titillating to imagine the world 200 years from now; thrilling to imagine further, 500 years from now; and this may then lure us to imagine 700 or even 1000 years hence – but where do we stop? If we follow this dynamic what is to keep us from imagining something utterly wild, such as, say, the year 802,701? That way madness lies. Yet that is precisely the year to which Wells's Time Traveller went right at the start of time-machine literature – and by the end of Wells's novel he went a good deal further than that, 30 million years into the future. [13] It may not be coincidence that one of the most famous works of nineteenth-century literature exploring the psychological dynamics of insanity, Nikolai Gogol's 'Diary of a Madman' (1835), includes the motif of dates expanding into hitherto unimagined quantities and shapes: after a sequence of diary entries moving in conventional fashion from October to December, a milestone in the protagonist's mental break-down is reached with the sudden appearance of an entry dated 'The Year 2000, 43rd of April'.[14] Gogol's fictional madman has an uncanny precursor in late poems by Friedrich Hölderlin (1770–1843), composed in the 1840s long after his full mental collapse, which he signed with the name 'Scardanelli' and to which he attached outlandish dates (1743, 1648, 1940 ...). [15] The ability to imagine any date whatsoever presupposes the loss of all binding reference points.

In other words, time machines in literature present a motif where the ideals of technology, science and rationality can suddenly transform into their opposites: absurdity, delusion and madness. Here we can perceive another facet of that strange scene in *Newton's Brain* where the inventor suddenly

13   During his frenzied first journey to the future Wells's Time Traveller says, 'with a kind of madness growing upon me, I flung myself into futurity'; H. G. Wells, *The Time Machine*, ed. by Stephen Arata (New York: Norton, 2009), p. 18.

14   Nikolai Gogol, 'The Diary of a Madman', in T*he Collected Tales of Nikolai Gogol*, trans. by Richard Pevear and Larissa Volokhonsky (New York: Vintage, 1998), p. 294.

15   See Friedrich Hölderlin, *Sämtliche Werke, Kritische Textausgabe*, Vol. 9: *Dichtungen nach 1806–Mündliches*, ed. by D. E. Sattler (Darmstadt and Neuwied: Luchterhand, 1984), pp. 69–91.

lifts off part of his skull 'like a cap', displays his bared brain, and calmly announces that his head in fact contains the looted brain of Isaac Newton. This scene is perverse, but it also anticipates the casual yet disturbing absurdities of twentieth-century Surrealism. It might go too far to claim Arbes's novella as an early work of modernist fiction, but certain lines of connection are undeniable. [16]

As an author exploring this ambiguous, shared ground between science fiction, tales of the perverse, and proto-modernist irrationalism, the figure to whom Arbes might most naturally be compared is Edgar Allan Poe. This is no coincidence: Arbes was a deep admirer of Poe and was the primary mediator of Poe's influence within Czech literature, translating a number of Poe's works and writing several studies of his life and work in the 1860s and 1870s. (Arbes was a great admirer of Gogol as well.) One of Arbes's best and most influential works is his 1873 novella *Saint Xavier*, a classic of later nineteenth-century Czech prose and one of the foundational works in the tradition of the 'Prague text' (in which the history, architecture, and haunting atmosphere of the ancient city figure as prominent themes). It was also directly inspired by Poe's famous tale of treasure and cryptography, 'The Gold-Bug' (1843).[17] Poe's influence was a major factor in the development of Arbes's

---

16   Tung argues for a fundamental interconnection of time machines as literary trope and literary modernism as such, in that both engage in 'radical rethinking of the shapes of time, the consistency of timespace and the nature of history', and envisage a 'pluralisation of time's speed, shape and lines of occurrence'; Tung, *Modernism and Time Machines*, pp. 4 and 3.

17   For a comparative analysis of Poe's 'The Gold-Bug' and Arbes's *Saint Xavier*, see Peter Zusi, 'Gold-Bugs and False Gemstones: Hermeneutics, Ekphrasis, and Coincidence in Edgar Allan Poe and Jakub Arbes', *Modern Language Review*, 117.3 (2022), 325–51.

distinctive genre, a subset of the novella to which he gave the name *romanetto*. This name, which he devised together with his friend and erstwhile teacher Jan Neruda (1834–1891, best known for his 1878 *Povídky malostranské*, 'Tales of the Lesser Quarter', another foundational Prague text) was intentionally exotic sounding, seeming more a term from a Romance language than anything Czech. Arbes's *romanettos* – which inspired a few significant disciples among later Czech authors but did not found a lasting literary form – combined elements of mystery, intrigue, and scientific or natural curiosities with attention to questions of social injustice and pronounced scepticism regarding the 'progress' achieved by modern European civilization.[18] Arbes had gained prominence as a journalist before becoming known for his fiction, and as an ardent advocate for social as well as 'national' equality – it must be remembered that Bohemia at this time was still part of the Habsburg Empire, with its administrative and cultural centre in Vienna, and the movement to achieve greater parity among Czech- and German-speakers in what we today know as the Czech Republic was fervid – had got into trouble many times with the authorities. Parts of his early *romanettos* were written in Habsburg prison cells. In line with this more sobering aspect of Arbes's writing, the suggestion of supernatural or fantastic events in his *romanettos* was always (as in the early Gothic

---

18 An earlier English translation of *Newton's Brain*, unfortunately containing lamentable inaccuracies and omissions, appeared in an 1897 collection titled *Clever Tales*, edited by Charlotte Parker and Helen A. Clarke (Boston: Copeland and Day). The volume also contains tales by August Strindberg, Villiers de l'Isle Adam, Vsevolod Garshin and Ludovic Halévy, which gives a sense of the literary company that the American editors (best known for founding *Poet Lore* in 1889, the oldest continuous poetry journal in the United States and an early venue for comparative literary study) felt was appropriate for Arbes.

fictions of Ann Radcliffe) resolved at the end through rational explanation. Arbes was not one to indulge in intentional mystification or facile escapism.

Indeed, the ending of *Newton's Brain* pulls back and brackets its audacious tale with an explanation that may strike modern readers as disappointing. Arbes seems to retreat from his tale of a time *machine* back into some of the narrative clichés that were discussed above as characterizing many tales of time *travel*: we can thus regard *Newton's Brain* as exemplifying that gradual transition from the latter to the former as literary motif. Without spoiling the ending for first-time readers, I would nonetheless suggest that it is more layered than it may initially appear, as in certain respects it touches on the themes of consciousness, imagination and narrative mentioned at the beginning of this introduction. Whatever judgment a reader might reach as to whether the conclusion is satisfying, there can be little doubt that its proffered explanations are not terribly convincing. Close attention to the details of the story raises too many unanswered questions, and the possibility that delusion or deliberate deception (but whose?) has been at work from the start is never entirely dispelled. In any event the reader's experience of the time-machine narrative, the Surreal events, and the troubling scenes of human aggression cannot be undone. Arbes provides no closure. This early work of Science Fiction, simultaneously thought-provoking, entertaining and disturbing, deserves greater recognition and a modern readership.

Highgate, September 2023

Jakub Arbes

Newton's Brain

Brain

A Romanetto

There are more things in heaven and earth, Horatio,
Than are dreamt of in our philosophy.
Hamlet

Before my God, I might not this believe
Without the sensible and true avouch
Of mine own eyes.
Horatio

I HAVE A WHIMSICAL TALE TO TELL, starting beside a grave... This is cynical of me, though I insist that, after a few words of explanation, even the most delicate of souls will forgive me... By its severe and unforgiving nature science has deprived many of us of the sweetest dream of our lifetime. Its ruthless hand has ripped open the veil – for the optimist seemingly transparent, for the pessimist eternally opaque – which hides what lies beyond the grave of living beings, and anyone who attaches greater faith to the rationalities of science than to traditional assumptions, be they ever so endearing, is faced with a prospect that is more or less clear, albeit terrifying.

So why should we grieve over the grave of one who believed, nay, was convinced, that all those matters that have filled us with bliss or with distress come to an end at death?

Why bemoan the death of one to whom sorrow had been more baneful than the most venomous sheer, who, loathing all misery and tears from the bottom of his heart, knew no sweeter sensation than that which prompts in man the realisation that his every endeavour has been directed towards banishing that most fell demon of the human soul – sorrow?

A man may have loved living more than this human life really merits, and he may have despised it as it truly deserves, and, not treating it seriously enough, underestimated it; however, to stand wailing over the grave of one who would have stood over his own grave erect, wearing the expression of a stoic and humorist and with his soul completely at ease, would surely be an unforgivable profanation of his memory.

The man of whom I speak was my friend from earliest childhood, and he died – or more properly fell – at the Battle of Sadowa as an officer in the Prince Constantine infantry regiment. His skull had been split in two by a Prussian pallasch...

His father had been head gardener to the Kinskys, whose gardens extended across the south-eastern slope of Petřín Hill in Prague, above the Újezd Gate.

We were distantly related, and although my friend came from a fairly prosperous family and my own family was very poor, we had been the closest of friends for almost twenty years. As children we would frolic together in their large grounds, and as teenagers we were at school together. Our lives, no less than our studies, were just as bizarre as our inclinations. For initially we were interested in everything that "came our way", picking over, scrutinising and analysing anything and everything that fate randomly cast before us.

We had lively debates, even fierce and passionate. Exchanging strange, often bizarre views was a constant attraction, and barely a day passed without our launching into a discussion of something or other that struck us as utterly insoluble. This uncontrolled, even frivolous hopping from one thing to another served no practical purpose, but at least it refined our dialectics and fired our imaginations, which subsequently produced quite wondrously bizarre outcomes.

To our fathers' no small dismay, neither I nor my friend made particularly good progress at school. On the other hand, in our "private" studies, that's to say in the sciences that we later embraced in full, we were streets ahead of our classmates.

And exactly as we had been endowed by Nature – I was born hideous, my friend handsome – so she inspired each of us with our particular inclinations: I leaned towards dreary, tiring and rarely amusing mathematics, he to the fresh and elevating natural sciences.

However, any strictly scientific leanings eluded us by such a distance that I really don't know whether to treat what we studied back then as pointless or as merely quirky.

Only my friend's studies had any practical, actually impishly practical success and purpose: mostly he studied physics, chemistry, mechanics and some branches of the other sciences for the purpose of what? – Doing magic tricks.

God alone knows where he got the idea that he was extraordinarily gifted for doing magic, but ever since he acquired that peculiar proclivity he showed no interest in anything that didn't tally in some way or other with it.

For sure, his father had no inkling of any of this, because my friend did everything in secret. I was his sole confidant, and it was in my student garret that all manner of experiments were conducted. My friend would spend every penny he came by on the purchase of books and instruments allied to every kind of wizardry, and they were all kept in my garret for safekeeping.

By the time several years had passed my little room had garnered such a collection of strange instruments that it came almost to resemble an alchemist's workshop.

It should be pointed out that my friend's progress on the magic front was amazingly rapid and quite astonishing, evidence of his truly extraordinary gift and of the passion with which he pursued his whim.

The more he thrived on his "pseudoscience", the greater his passion grew, so it frequently came about that while I was slogging away, calculating how high a balloon weighing such and such and filled with such and such a gas would have to fly in such and such conditions, my friend, under the same roof and only feet away from me, was repeating for the thousandth time in a row an utterly trivial experiment aimed at finding how it might be possible for a card to be played that anyone might have indicated but a moment before.

My friend would use my room to practice in my absence, and then he'd pull many a trick on me later.

However, he kept certain particularly interesting experiments even from me. He might drop the odd hint that he had something in the making, things that would surprise those who knew, and he could explain even the most admired tricks by the most renowned purveyors of magic, but without ever revealing their true essence.

In the company of friends, he frequently demonstrated his credibility by means of genuinely surprising experiments. There was nothing superficial about what he did and he was quite dismissive of common or garden sleight of hand. That had merely been the necessary antecedent to his acquisition of the requisite dexterity. His ambition was to exploit the sciences to his own advantage.

His secret quest was for just the right synthesis and integration of various mechanical, physical and chemical effects; statics and dynamics, hydro- and aerostatics, hydro- and aerodynamics, optics with its offshoots of dioptrics and catoptrics, acoustics, magnetism, electricity, synthetic and analytical chemistry – all of these and parts of other sciences as well, such as astronomy, anatomy, physiology etc., were sifted through over the course of seven or eight years with consummate industry and care. But all with an eye to working magic.

Nor is it at all surprising that my friend bought, whatever the cost, every available book not only on magic tricks, but also on such other topics as wizardry, alchemy, astrology, mesmerism and somnambulism, mysticism, chiromancy, theosophy, geomancy, prognostics, physiognomy and suchlike.

My friend's library, kept like all his paraphernalia in my garret, was the weirdest hotchpotch.

Side by side with books of genuine scientific value by such recognised authorities as Newton, Linnaeus, Locke, Leibniz, Bacon, François Arago, Wolf, Lavoisier, Descartes, Robert Brown, Mohs, Cuvier, Humboldt and others, you might find such books by unknown or forgotten pseudo-scientists and charlatans as Paracelsus' *Zwölff Bücher, darin alle gehaimnüß der natur eröffnet*, published in 1570 in Strasburg, Mehun's *Mirror of Alchimy*, Mayer's *Letters for a Higher Truth, from Manuscripts Relating to Magnetism,* Böckmann's *Archive for Magnetism and Somnambulism*, published at the end of last century, Cagliostro's *Adventures*, Commiers' *Les oracles des sibylles*, published about a century ago, Crusius' work on Schroepfer's method of exorcism, Wincer's *Demonology*, de Luchet's *Essais sur la secte des Illuminés*, Gall's works on phrenology and Lavater's on physiognomy, Megphilos' *Miracles and Mysteries of the Spirit World*, Magikon's *Archive of Noology and the Magnetic Life*, the *Turba philosophorum*, published by Morgenstern in 1613, that is, the *Auriferae artis, quam chemiam vocant antiquissimi authores*, which deals with the earliest philosophy, universal therapy, the philosopher's stone, alchemy, etc., the *Reports on Ancient and Modern Mysteries*, the

Onomastologia curiosa or Lexicon of Natural Magic, published in Nuremberg in 1764, and other like things.

Mr friend did not let himself be misled by most of these writings, not in the least.

His clear intellect soared above such a plethora of mental aberrations, and, relying on the achievements of science, he troubled himself with all these preparatory studies more out of curiosity than necessity, though he made no secret of the fact that in practical terms a knowledge of these mental aberrations might well contribute to the enhancement of natural deceptions.

Accordingly, my friend pursued his subject not only with industry and zeal, but also independently.

Not only did he teach himself additional, previously known experiments from his books of magic and mystery, but he also, on the basis of the knowledge he had acquired, tinkered and experimented independently, in a word, he operated systematically, seeking to ground his "pseudoscience" on as broad and as solid foundations as possible.

No surprise, then, that when he later gave practical performances, he frequently exceeded the expectations of all those present.

His agreeable exterior, his sophisticated, deft reasoning, his ready, even sarcastic wit, and his technical dexterity acquired by long years' practice, all came to his aid during the most demanding demonstrations.

As evidence of the dexterity that he had acquired, let me mention just a few of the many hundreds of more or less familiar, and unfamiliar, demonstrations that I saw with my own eyes.

Swallowing burning pitch and pebbles, reeling bootlaces and ribbons out of his mouth, thrusting knives into his breast or swallowing needles, knives and swords are mostly more in the realm of tacky conjuring, but my friend was as good at these and other similar things as any star performer admired across the land.

My friend once performed a neat, original experiment at the wedding breakfast of one of my relatives.

We were seated at a long table in the middle of a spacious room. There were twelve of us in all. At the centre of the table sat the bride, beside her the groom, then the bridesmaid and best man. I was sitting opposite the bridesmaid, my friend at the other end of the table, roughly two metres from the bride.

Our spirits were high. The food was plentiful and excellent, the mood ever more jocund. Before long, the conversation was totally dominated by jokes and jollity.

As the meal was drawing to a close, a huge, deep bowl of boiled crayfish was brought to the table and set down before the bride. She, however, whether as none too keen herself on the dish, or from consideration, bade the groom to pass it on.

The groom did as bidden, and so the bowl passed from hand to hand until it came back to the bride, by now almost empty. It goes without saying that all that was left were tiny little things, everyone having taken the biggest ones.

The dear bride, noting that the groom had not yet had any of the crayfish, was keen to choose for him at least one or two of the largest ones remaining; bending her head, she directed her ferreting blue eyes into the bowl and grabbed the largest one with her little alabaster hand.

However, she had hardly placed it on the groom's plate when she started and with a squeak of horror shrank back from the table – staring back out at her from the bowl were the bright eyes of what? – a disgusting frog...

"What's that?" the groom cried and, grabbing a fork, he jabbed at the creature.

The latter hopped out of the bowl right in front of the bride.

All the guests evinced their surprise; only my friend, sitting calmly at the other end of the table, remarked:

"Why are you stabbing the poor thing?"

Then he rose and touched the frog, which jumped over the bride's head in the direction of the door.

Leaping to his feet, the groom stamped on the frog with one foot, and to the no small amazement of all, the frog wailed, in a human voice: "Woe is me! That's me done for!"

The groom jumped back and my friend bent down to the floor and picked up not a frog, but a snow-white lady's glove.

Then taking the bride's handkerchief, he wrapped the glove in it, placed the package in front of the bride and mumbled, as the renowned Bosco used to mumble, the Italian exorcism formula: *"Spiriti miei ubbidite!"*

Then when one of the guests unwrapped the handkerchief, it was found to contain some expensive gold earrings, my friend's present to the bride.

To have had a sparrow, pigeon, hare, mole or some other small animal declared dead, then to take a penknife and carefully remove its brain from its skull, replace the brain with a sweet-smelling wad of cotton apparently soaked in some tincture, and then to bid the animal suddenly come back to life as if from a faint, then to have it hop up and fly or run away is a fairly familiar bit of trickery, but my friend had performed it in so many mutations that it captivated even those spectators who'd seen similar experiments countless times before.

He once conducted a truly original demonstration that spoke particularly of his intellectual dexterity.

We were sitting together in one of the most elegant inns in Prague at one end of a long table in the middle of the room.

All the tables along the walls were occupied. It was a summer's day, but overcast; it was raining outside and we two were feeling bored and a bit down in the mouth.

It wasn't long before a carriage trundled up outside the inn and a few minutes later a young couple, apparently newlyweds on honeymoon, entered.

They sat down at the other end of the table where we were sitting and the young husband ordered lunch for his dear wife and himself.

My friend, more sullen and tetchy than me, practically ignored the couple, whereas I could see very well how tender and thoughtful the newlyweds were being to each other, clear evidence that they'd only been married a few days, that they loved each other truly, deeply and sincerely, and that they were happy.

The young husband kept leaning across to his fair, rosy-cheeked young wife and whispering something to her – plainly various sweet nothings, because she always smiled a sweet smile.

They'd enjoyed their soup and were eating some beef. As they ate they showed each other every possible kindness, concern and solicitude.

They constantly asked each other whether they were enjoying their meal and whether they might not fancy this or that.

At first their conversation was conducted in a whisper and unintelligibly; later, having grown more used to the company among which they found themselves, they spoke louder and sometimes entirely intelligibly.

The only words I heard were filled with love and tenderness; both their voices often quivered with emotion, though the talk itself was entirely mundane.

"Are you watching them billing and cooing?" my friend whispered to me. "Half an hour from now, even sooner, they'll be up for a fight."

"That's not possible," I replied, also in a whisper.

"You'll see," he replied. "Let's ignore them, carry on with our own conversation, but keep one ear on theirs."

Agreeing to his suggestion, I then heard the following exchange:

He: "You're also glad that we're in Prague now, aren't you, Vendulka dear?"

She: "But of course! You wouldn't believe how happy I am to be able to be at your side and gaze at any moment into your eyes..." (In a muffled, somewhat dark tone: "If only it weren't for your infidelities!")

He: "My infidelities? Where did you get that from, sugar-plum?"

She: "Where did I get what from? Nothing, I got nothing!... But you... What do you mean? What infidelities?"

He: "Me? It was you who said it!"

She: "I never said a word..."

He: "Come, come, you little rascal – I heard it with my own ears: 'If only it weren't for your infidelities!'"

She: "It was you said that, not me..."

He: "Ridiculous – I never said a thing..."

She: "Oh, you can't talk me out of what I know I heard – " (tearfully): "I don't deserve to be charged with infidelity." (In a muffled, somewhat dark tone: "It's scandalous to accuse me of infidelity with the whole world talking about yours.")

He and She (simultaneously): "My infidelity?"

He: "Who's had the gall?"

She: "It's a slur!"

He: "And you can accuse me of something like that here, in a public place?"

She: "But I never said a thing – it's you accusing me! – "

He: "Nothing could be further from my mind!"

She (tearfully): "This is too much!" (In a muffled tone: "Ugh, how can you!")

He (drawing himself up somewhat and casting her an angry look): "Don't go creating a scene in public – the whole place is staring at us..."

I looked around.

The young husband was right. Most of the patrons really were watching the newlyweds, who in such a sudden, odd and rather confused way had started accusing each other of infidelity.

It was plain to see that both were embarrassed, trying to conceal their anger and indignation, but to no avail: the exchange continued as it had begun, with ever greater vigour and passion.

Every now and then yet another muffled inanity could be heard coming from the wife's lips – then he'd charge her with it, she'd deny having said anything of the kind, insisting that the offending words had been uttered by him, while he swore by all that's holy that it was not he.

This peculiar dispute between the two ever more agitated and indignant young people went on for almost half an hour.

The young wife went at her spouse with increasing violence, while he grew ever gloomier, angrier and more reproachful – but to no avail! The edge of her tongue grew ever sharper and more scathing until her young husband leapt to his feet as his outrage boiled over and raised a menacing hand against his poor little wife.

At that instant, however, my friend leapt to his feet, arrested the husband's hand and said:

"Be forgiving, dear sir – your wife is entirely innocent: this has all been just a simple, if ungentlemanly joke – she knows nothing..."

"How so?" the husband asked, surprised and in a somewhat irascible tone. "I know what I've been hearing..."

"True," said my friend, "but it wasn't the voice of your dear sweet lady wife, but mine..."

"How so? What are you trying to say?"

"Sir, I'm a ventriloquist and all the muffled words about infidelity and causing a scene, and all the inanities that you, and your wife, heard and which you thought were being said by her while she's been attributing them to you – all those words that caused the confusion were uttered by me. It is, then for me to crave your forgiveness and I insist that you do indeed forgive this unusual, though actually innocent little jest."

The young husband and his wife were initially so confused that they didn't know whether to believe what my friend had said or not; but then he produced several more soothing and apologetic words, partly in the husband's voice, as if he was speaking from the cellar, partly in the wife's, as if it was coming down from the ceiling, so they did both believe him and, looking reconciled, forgave the jest…

From what I have just said of my friend's skill and virtuosity with his "pseudoscience" – a full account of his repertoire would more than fill a very fat book – it follows that he could compete without fear against the most adroit tricksters ever to appear in public. However, from the outset his main focus had been on "citing the spirits".

The apparatus and other devices that he employed in the process he kept even from me. He did once ask if I'd like to see a person from history, and said he would cite them. I named Napoleon I.

Several nights passed without Napoleon appearing to me, but once, after I'd forgotten all about my friend's promise, I was roused from my slumber, in the night, by a gentle tap on the door.

Sitting upright in bed, I rubbed my eyes. But because the tapping was repeated, I asked: "Who's there?"

Instead of a reply, the door opened gently and with stately step in walked Napoleon I as I'd seen him portrayed any number of times – grey coat, white trousers, high riding boots and that historic three-cornered hat.

Without a word, he walked slowly over to the window and then back to the door.

I wanted to address the vision, but I didn't – and I would stress how odd it is that to this day I don't know why I didn't.

I witnessed many more demonstrations of this kind. Whenever I asked my friend for some such thing, he would invariably put if off until he had all the requisite props and even greater finesse.

He also told me on many an occasion that he was working on the construction of strange, automated, contraptions with which he wanted to perform actual "miracles" and fool whole companies of scholars and experts.

At some later stage he meant to invite a large number of friends and devotees of this type of entertainment and execute several kinds of the most contrived and so most mystifying fabrications.

He would assure me how surprised I was going to be, and from what I had witnessed previously I could be confident that he would be as good as his word.

Thus did we live and study for a number of years. Our initially wide-ranging, but later one-sided studies had their repercussions.

Shortly before 1860 we failed our end-of-year exams so stunningly that any thought of re-sitting them after the summer holidays was utterly pointless. So we repeated the year and failed again, and a year later, yet again. My friend's father, who had often jokingly threatened his son that if he didn't do well at school he'd have him apprenticed to a cobbler, finally lost patience, and after an exhaustive family conference it was decreed that it would be best if my friend joined the army.

My friend raised no objections and shortly after that he came to see me clad in the uniform of a cadet of the Royal and Imperial Prince Constantine of Russia Infantry Regiment.

"Well – how about you?" he began, offering me his hand.

"I've taken up carpentry."

"For a lifetime?"

"I don't know. I'm in training, or rather, they've got me down as a trainee, but I've yet to lay hands on an adze."

"And maybe you never will," the novitiate of the blood-and-guts brigade said, laughing.

"Maybe," I replied. "But we could be in the same boat: you might never again lay hands on some of your magic paraphernalia."

"Far from it! That's why I'm here. I want to relieve you of all my junk; you can scarcely move an inch in this poky little room of yours."

"Fine. But where shall we put it all?"

"Tomorrow or the day after I'll have some crates delivered – you can help me and we'll stow it all away. I'll have the crates taken, without anyone knowing, to the cellars of the Prince's chateau, and in the event..., I mean, whenever I start getting bored in Trieste or Pest or some Catholic village in the Tyrol..., well, I'll drop you a line, you can dig out the items I need and send them to me."

I promised I would.

And next day we filled no less than five crates with books, apparatus and microscope slides, in short, every conceivable item of a magician's tackle.

The day after, my friend had the crates taken away.

We did see each other a couple more times, but a fortnight or so later he received the order to repair to his regimental depot at Königgrätz.[19]

Thereafter I was on my own. My friend didn't write to me, nor I to him, and so ended the once indivisible friendship between us, though any indifference was merely apparent.

---

19   On this and other Czech place names see the Postscript.

TWO YEARS LATER – something tells me it was in January or February 1866 – my friend did get back in touch, and with a fairly long letter.

It was full of all kinds of ripping yarns of army life, and he also mentioned his "craze" for magic tricks. He bade me write back soon and tell him how life had been treating me, ending his letter thus:

> *You know the expression 'What a lark!'? If you don't, you'd certainly get the full idea of it if you were an officer in the same regiment as me. I couldn't wish for any jollier, more good-humoured comrades, a more carefree existence...*
>
> *Except that sometimes – only some of the time, see? – when the end of the month is approaching and the last pay packet is out of the window..., I get really down in the dumps...*
>
> *Several times I've thought of finding a way out, but have never done it...*
>
> *And so I'm writing to ask you this: if you happen to know of anyone who's as crazy now as I used to be all those years ago, write and tell me – they might care to buy all, or at least some, of the magic paraphernalia that I've got stored in the cellars of the Kinskys' villa in Smíchov.*

I hadn't expected the letter to end like that.

Knowing my friend's passion for his beloved pseudoscience, I couldn't believe he could have wrenched himself so totally free of it, and assuming that the above words in his letter were either a sudden whim, or, more likely, just another bit of pure hocus-pocus – having me think that he'd given up his pseudo-science altogether – I simply replied that I knew no one who would want to buy that which he was offering for sale.

At least partial evidence that I hadn't been mistaken was my friend's second letter, in reply to mine.

He was at great pains to explain that despite his every effort to forget his magic mania, the sole option left to him had been to see if he could kill off his passion by selling all his trappings; though the moment he'd posted that first letter, he bitterly regretted writing it, adding that if a buyer should happen along, he wasn't going to sell after all.

At the end of the letter he said that in idle moments he still toyed with the idea of constructing his automated contraptions, assuring me that if it ever came to a show involving them, it would be spectacular...

Shortly before war was declared between Prussia and Austria I received another letter from my friend – his last. Again it was written in an airy, even impish tone; I take the following extract from it:

> *A few days from now, we might be ordered onto the battlefield. Pity your poor friend...*
>
> *Without my apparatus and my microscope slides, without my playing cards and mirrors, without my tinctures and all the other essentials, I shall have to mutter 'Spiriti miei ubbidite' and my previously ever-obedient and up-for-any-thing 'spirits' may for the first time decline to obey...*

Amid a hail of bullets, a simple bit of lead is more powerful than all incantations, and my own sabre and revolver may yet help many to an early acquaintanceship with the mysterious idea that no human power...

Ah, what's the point in getting bogged down in sentimentality!... Sooner or later each of us will come to know – as the billions of creatures who have preceded us came to know – whether life does end with death or not... So why bother philosophising?...

And as the last cruel fight comes nigh – maybe I'll plead 'Spiriti miei ubbidite', or maybe I shall keep silent and not even remember my 'spiriti'...

But I do have one favour to ask: If I do fall in battle – mourn thou not! Call all our old friends together and remember me over brimming glasses!...

If you fulfil this last wish of mine, you may be sure that I shall visit you again, at least once...

Having read these closing lines, I smiled, the way we smile at a paradox...

Since that letter, I heard no more of my friend, until after the Battle of Sadowa.

For it was then that I received, by post, so probably the last posting before all postal communication was interrupted, a note that read as follows:

> *Dear Sir,*
> *A young officer has just been brought to our town, a first lieutenant of the Königgrätz regiment. He is seriously wounded; his skull has been split open and he is in a coma.*

He was found only today, about an hour away from here, in a gully at the edge of a small wood to which he appears to have dragged himself after being wounded.

As I write, he remains to be identified, however I hope this will happen today or tomorrow.

I learned your address from a letter found on his person and am sending you this sad news in order that you may inform the injured man's relatives and friends as to his whereabouts.

Respectfully yours
Fr Vojtěch Nosal
Parish priest, Nechanitz

At that moment it wasn't particularly easy or pleasant to travel to areas occupied by the Prussian army, but that notwithstanding, I decided forthwith to go to Nechanitz.

Having written a brief note to my friend's father, enclosing the Nechanitz priest's letter, I departed without waiting for confirmation that my letter had been delivered by its messenger, taking the train as far as Neu-Kolin, to which it was still running, then hiring a cart to Nechanitz.

I reached Nechanitz at gone two in the morning.

At the edge of the town my cart was stopped by a Prussian patrol. I told them where I was going and why, and the patrol NCO ordered one of his men to accompany me to the rectory and wait there until I was admitted.

In only a few minutes my cart was in the square, outside the rectory. I hopped down, rang the bell and moments later the little gate was opened.

Here, too, I explained why I had come, and was duly admitted into the yard, while my carter was told to drive into the yard by the rear gate.

The man who had opened the gate led me inside the house and, having assured me that he would inform the priest, who had just come back from seeing a dying Saxon officer lying with many other injured men inside the church, he went.

I was left in the ante-room for just moments before a side door creaked and the priest came in, lantern in hand.

He greeted me amiably and just as amiably brushed aside my apology for disturbing him at such an unearthly hour, then he took me upstairs, where he had his living room and several other rooms adapted to receiving the wounded.

"He has yet to be identified," said the priest as he opened the living room door, "but I hope you'll recognise him."

We entered the room, which was sunk in gloom.

Twenty or so privates were lying along the wall on improvised beds on the ground; several beds with the seriously wounded were disposed closer to the windows.

The priest led me over to one of them and silently raised his lantern.

I looked into the injured man's pale, even livid features, his head swathed in ice, and recognised my friend instantly.

He was still unconscious, lying there motionless with his eyes half-closed and his laboured breathing the only sign of life.

"It's been three days now," the priest whispered to me, "since he was brought here, and the doctors have given up all hope. They recommend ice to his head and quinine, otherwise just rest..."

I wanted to say something to my friend, but seeing his desperate condition I turned to leave.

We left the living room.

Out in the corridor, having thanked the priest for his kindness, I made to leave, but he kindly invited me to stay as his guest at least until the morning. Being fit to drop, I gladly accepted the invitation and went into the ground-floor guest room.

"Do you happen to know, Father, anything more about my friend's injury?" I asked after we'd sat down at the large table in the spacious room.

"Amid all the chaos there's been during the last few days," the priest began, "it's been hard to find out anything of substance. Beyond a few details garnered from what the less seriously wounded have said, we still know very little about the dreadful battle of July 3rd.

"Your friend's regiment fought at Gitschin, where, however, it got split up. One section began retreating towards Smirschitz, the other, larger section headed south and was assigned to the first army corps. On July 3rd, that section was among the first army corps' reserves and was apparently sent around four in the afternoon to support those fighting near Problus.

"And it was there that your friend was injured. To judge from his wound, he was hit with a pallasch just as he'd bent down to pick something up, because the upper part of his skull has been almost completely chipped off. Your friend's injury is fatal and all the doctors who've examined it have been very surprised that he's still alive."

Hardly had the priest stopped speaking when the door opened. One of the men tending the wounded entered and whispered something to him.

A sad glance from the clergyman triggered my involuntary question:

"Dead, is he?"

"Dead," the priest repeated gloomily.

We went back up to the sitting room. My friend lay there, stretched out on his bed and uncovered. His once fair, youthful features now wore an expression of unutterable pain.

"He'll have to be buried this very morning," the priest pointed out.

I went up close to the bed and touched my friend's hand. It was already cold as ice.

My eyes filled with tears... I turned aside and, unable to utter a word, accompanied the priest back downstairs.

The first glimmering of dawn was coming in through the windows. Leaving me in the first room, the priest took himself off to his bedroom... I lay down on the sofa in my clothes, but with nary a hope of dropping off to sleep...

About two hours later a hubbub broke out in the yard. I got up, crossed the room back and forth and waited in almost feverish agitation...

The moment came.

After nine o'clock, the joint funeral of all the soldiers who had succumbed to their injuries in the night was held.

I accompanied my friend on his final journey. I saw him lowered into his grave..., and, devastated, I immediately set off back to Prague.

Now, following years in which I'd so often been witness to the cruel, inexorable rampaging of death among the ranks of the living, to how suddenly and ruthlessly its icy breath can often get the better of beings bubbling over with vitality – now I would certainly have taken my friend's death, in the spirit of his wishes and conviction, as a welcome release from the pain and misery which Providence has so generously lavished on us mortals.

However, at the time, I was still young, so at an age when the death of a dear one makes a huge impression even on one less sensitive than I had been, and so it is no surprise that the effect on me of my friend's death was nothing short of crushing.

At first, it didn't seem possible that my friend really had died.

But when, in moments of seclusion, I brought to mind all the details, when I vividly reminded myself that no grave ever gives up that which it has taken to its bosom, when I became engrossed in the thought of never, never ever, seeing my friend again, that he was now lost forever to me as for anyone else, I was repeatedly seized by a sense of unutterable bitterness.

And yet, at each recollection of my friend, I couldn't help remembering the words of his last letter:

> *If I fall in battle – mourn thou not! Call all our old friends together and remember me over brimming glasses!...*

I felt obliged to fulfil this last wish of his, though in the early days I was prevented from doing so by my pain and grief.

Shortly after my friend's departure for Königgrätz, I had given up my traineeship and gone back to studying, eagerly, redoubling my efforts with the determination to make up all that I had neglected during my one-sided studies of years before.

Then after my friend's death my zeal for studying reached, to all appearances, its peak. I studied in a feverish thrill; yet despite all this, not even the most strenuous mental effort could banish memories of my friend, especially the thought that I was sinning against our friendship by not fulfilling his final wish.

Almost four months passed after my friend's death; autumn had arrived and only now did I take the plunge and set about fulfilling that wish.

Choosing the evening of the last day of October, I called together all our old friends and a handful of acquaintances to the tavern in Prague's Kleinseite, a small one, but renowned for its wine, where, years before, we'd enjoyed many a lively interlude.

However, having arrived at the tavern rather late in the evening, I found that of the twelve people invited none apart from myself had shown up.

Saddened, I sat down at the table where, years before, we had been wont to sit, ordered myself a bottle of the best Žernoseky and lost myself in thought.

The pub was quite deserted.

Accordingly I was able to think undisturbed, and I did think, of friendship and loyalty, life and death and Lord knows what else...

My thoughts and reminiscences were gloomy, bitter, even painful. No surprise then, that one of the most vivid memories was of my late friend.

The image of him thrust itself upon me quite distinctly, though not nearly so as four months previously as I was leaving Nechanitz... It had begun to fade... and the idea that it would fade away completely, that I would perhaps be unable one day to call up even a single feature of his face, produced an unutterable bitterness in my soul...

Never!...

For the first time in my life I appreciated the profound and no less horrific import of this simple word, uttered countless times a day...

Never again to see a congenial face, never again press a dear hand – never – never!...

The longer I mused upon the significance of this fateful word, the sadder, the more hopeless were the thoughts that swirled about inside my head.

However, the cause of my gloomy thoughts were not so much the circumstances that had given rise to them, but above all and beyond any doubt my mental decrepitude.

For I had been studying so hard of late that I barely left my garret for a whole fortnight.

Anyone who has personal experience of the stifling malaise that desolates the human spirit after a long period of mental stress will fully understand my state of mind at that time.

For several months I'd been chiefly engaged in optics and applied mathematics with particular regard to astronomy; but my studies hadn't progressed as I wished and my soul was still dominated by the chaos that inevitably precedes the ultimate crystallisation of the more important principles of this or that science.

No surprise, then, that in this peculiar frame of mind I'd begun to reach for a glass more often than usual, and no surprise either that I left the tavern sooner than I'd intended, and that I found myself back in my garret in a much worse mood than that in which I'd left it.

I collapsed, worn out, on the chair at my desk.

I reached at random into the bookcase for a book and, opening it, was about to start reading.

But having read barely half a page, I thrust the book aside, propped my head in both hands and started to think. This thinking soon changed into meditation and that in turn into a half-slumber...

Suddenly I thought I heard the distant rumble of a carriage.

I looked up and listened.

I was surrounded by a deathly silence, while, outside, the autumn wind gave the odd painful and impassioned wail. The rumble was getting ever closer until it appeared that the carriage had stopped outside the house in which I was living.

I made to rise and glance out of the window, but, overcome by fatigue, I stemmed my curiosity and calmly remained seated.

Then I heard someone ring the concierge's bell and in due course the front door opening and closing.

Actually no one living in the house could possibly be arriving home in a carriage, but the human voices, notably that of the concierge, which I could make out, were evidence that the arrival was someone entitled to enter.

A few moments later, my drowsiness got the better of me again.

How long I dozed I cannot say, but I was roused from my slumber by a faint tap on the door.

I looked up again and listened.

Before me on the table the lamp was burning, casting its lustreless yellowish light about the room. The deathly quiet reigned again.

But what was that?

I heard the tap on the door again and quite clearly.

"Come in!" I said faintly.

The handle clicked and the door opened softly. In the gloom of the doorway I saw a slim male figure. I was about ten steps away from it and couldn't make out any of its facial features or what it was wearing.

"Who's that? And what do you seek at this late hour?" I asked the motionless figure in the doorway.

Instead of replying, the figure nudged the door wide open and the yellowish gleam of the lamp lit it up...

I let out a shriek of terror and tried to leap up, but my legs failed me.

There in the doorway stood... my friend...

The deathly hush reigned a few moments longer.

Without uttering a word, my friend stood there, motionless, while I was unable to tear my gaze from him.

His face was deathly pale, but his clear, blue eyes radiated life and a light, amiable smile played about his lips.

"Good evening," he said after a while and took several steps forward.

Catching the clink of a sabre I registered that he was wearing an officer's uniform.

"You aren't dead?" I spluttered when he'd come to within three steps of me.

"How could I be dead if I'm standing here in front of you?" he came back with his clear, pleasant voice.

"Am I dreaming or am I awake?" I struggled to enunciate. "Didn't I see you in Nechanitz, your head split open and dying, and later, dead?"

"You may have seen me, or you may have seen someone else," my unexpected guest replied. "But I'm standing before you now, hale and hearty – so there can be no doubt. My hand!"...

He offered me his hand.

Briefly I hesitated, but then I gave him mine and could feel his hand not cold, but warm, as it once used to be.

My bewilderment grew and grew. But in spite of everything I couldn't yet bring myself to believe that a few months previously I might have misidentified the person of my friend at Nechanitz.

"You acted on my last wish," my friend continued, after we had shaken hands, "and I'm being as good as my word..., I've come to visit you..."

"But how's this all possible?" I asked in disbelief.

"Quite simply," he replied. "Above all, do let me sit down, then I'll tell you all in a nutshell, I've got plenty of time to spare."

Silently I brought forward a chair and my friend sat down beside me.

"Well?" I enquired.

"At Nechanitz you probably saw an officer who resembles me. It was Lieutenant Jiruš, who was badly wounded near Poblus and died, as I learned later, in Nechanitz. The error could have happened simply because he looked like me. That's the whole miracle."

"But how could they have found on him a letter sent by me to you in which the Nechanitz priest found my address?"

"That's perfectly simple. For several hours before the battle, the greater part of our regiment was lying in reserve in a small wood. The men were battle-ready, only the officers were going from company to company or standing chatting in groups.

"You mustn't be thinking that light-hearted soldiery gets particularly serious before a battle; there's often joking during the bloodiest encounters, not to mention the time spent waiting impatiently before the order comes to march or fire.

"I well remember that that time I wasn't exactly in a mind for joking, but I was bored and fished out your letter to re-read it."

"Lieutenant Jiruš crept upon me unseen and thinking I was reading a love letter, whipped it out of my hands to read it aloud to our comrades. And at that moment came the order to march.

"Lieutenant Jiruš stuffed it in his pocket and hurried off to join his company, while I drew my sabre and joined my line, and a few moments later there was such a violent exchange of gunfire that my mind was focussed entirely on the enemy.

"How the battle ended, you know. I was captured and now I've just returned from Königsberg, where, it goes without saying, I was well and truly bored."

"Why didn't you drop me a line at least?" I asked, when he finished.

"Pure caprice," same the calm reply. "That apart, I was tormenting myself ad nauseam with studying mathematics and astronomy, following your example."

"But what brings you at such a late hour to me? – When did you get back?" I urged, by now almost persuaded that he was alive and well as before.

"I arrived this evening, but yesterday all our mutual friends knew I was coming, which is why they didn't come to the tavern where you'd invited them.

"You're the only one I didn't inform about my arrival, just to make the surprise all the greater. And now I'm here to invite you to the banquet my father is giving at the chateau Kinsky to mark my safe return.

"Most probably, all our friends and the other guests are already there – I just came away to collect you. And I can also tell you that I'm putting on the greatest trick show ever, which, as you know, I've been beavering away at for several years.

"The automated devices and all the necessary apparatus are in perfect condition and I insist that all of you who are going to be there will have a great time."

From all I'd just seen and heard it was obvious that I really had been visited by my supposedly dead friend, and that he hadn't changed one bit as regards his bizarre turn of mind.

"And what led you to hold the banquet today precisely? Couldn't it have waited?" I asked after a pause.

"Hold on!" my friend said. "It's my father who's organised it with the acquiescence of the Kinskys, who for their own part have also invited numerous guests. See how the chateau is all lit up for the occasion."

He then crossed to the window, from which part of the Kinsky house could be seen, and drew back the curtain. All the chateau windows were indeed lit up...

"The banquet began about an hour ago," he continued. "My performance will come later, which is why I came out to let you know. Come along if you want. But you'll have to come on foot, sorry! I have to get back straight away and without you – though purely for reasons connected with the show. So, will you come?"

"Yes," I said, rising.

Then he quickly stood up, gave me his hand and left.

I heard his footsteps retreating, I heard the street door open and close, then I caught the sound of someone banging a carriage door shut, and then the rumble of the carriage departing.

I listened as the rumble faded into the distance until it died.

Despite seeming so probable and plausible, all that I had just witnessed was so peculiar that I remained seated, motionless, incapable of gathering my senses.

It wasn't long before my incredulity reasserted itself.

Being alone there and not detecting any change around me, I almost thought that the whole thing had been but a dream. However, those lights on at the Kinsky chateau, which I had seen from the window, confirmed me in the belief that I had *not* been dreaming and that I could, indeed should, comply with my friend's desire.

The feeling that overcame me after my friend left will stay with me forever.

The sensation was so utterly agreeable, like that felt by one who has been unexpectedly relieved of the chimaera that has been pursuing him for a long, long time.

I felt an extraordinary sense of freshness and strength.

Wasting no more time musing, I tossed on my overcoat, grabbed my hat and left my room to itself.

I slowly descended the stairs, tapped on the concierge's window, had him open the door and went out into the street.

It was a bright, autumnal, moonlit night.

Half-hidden by a slight mist, the moon hung pensively over Petřín and by its silvery, somewhat blurry light the damp paving stones shone like the surface of a lake rippled by a gentle breeze.

A by now almost ice-cold north wind occasionally made itself felt. Since it was blowing right at me, I quickened my step and some fifteen minutes later found myself outside the grating of the entrance to the Kinsky garden.

The main gate was wide open, as was the little side gate, and the elderly porter, long known to me, wearing a fur coat as in the coldest of winters, was pacing about impatiently.

"Are there a lot of guests?" I asked him.

"Indeed so," came the muffled, somewhat sullen reply.

"And has the party begun?"

"Possibly, though I can't be absolutely sure. Young Lord Bedřich went out about half an hour ago and he's only just come back."

"What are they actually celebrating?"

"I couldn't say, but the young master, who we all thought dead, has returned, so it's probably in his honour..."

"So it's true!" I mumbled in spite of myself, finally convinced that what I had recently witnessed in my garret had not been an apparition, but the real thing.

"So it must be all right for me to go up as well, mustn't it?" I asked casually, knowing in advance that the old porter would have let me in even if he'd been specifically ordered to admit no uninvited guest.

"But I've got you right here, top of the guest list," came the reply.

"Good bye, then," I said and made my way up along the broad, sandy, gently sloping driveway.

Within the beautiful park, the cold of those autumn nights had already left visible signs of its inexorable, destructive power.

The leaves on trees and shrubs were already quite yellow and had mostly fallen; here and there, totally bare, dark branches of trees reared up high and in the pale lunar half-light their damp trunks, branches and leaves glistened in a range of wondrous shades of light.

The silence of the night was disturbed now and then by a waft of the cold north wind, which wailed beseechingly in the branches and here and there blew some of the damp fallen leaves a few steps on and then, with a faint whisper and rustle, suddenly died away in the distance.

Before long, I found myself at the spot from where, as recently as 1866, there had been an open panorama of the southern part of Prague.

A light mist was floating above the city, accompanied by the mysterious calm of the autumn night.

The sky was faint and little fluffy, greyish clouds were hurtling southwards, evidence that, high above, it was still windy. Now and again, the odd little cloud veiled the moon and its thin shadow scuttled across Prague as if hastening to reach the mystical realm of eternal oblivion.

I paused to take in the beautiful picture spread out before me.

I might have stood there longer, but suddenly, from somewhere in the heights, came the hollow hooting of an owl, and alone this sound of a vigilant living creature reminded me that I had reached my nocturnal destination.

I turned, quickened my pace and in moments there, about five hundred paces ahead of me, rose up the whitish contours of the prince's summer residence.

There were lights in all the windows and outside the house dark human figures flitted back and forth. A little further on I could see carriages waiting, as I had seen them many times in the past at various festivities.

After a short while I caught the muffled sound of music, apparently coming from the house.

I couldn't quite tell what kind of music it was, but it did strike me as not the riotously jolly kind heard at joyful celebrations, it was more sombre, sad, like a funeral march...

However, it soon fell silent, leaving audible only the crunching of sand beneath my feet. I quickened my pace even more.

The closer I got to the house, the fewer the dark human figures who had been flitting there previously, and when I eventually found myself right beside the building, the entire place was dead and deserted, as if the chateau were uninhabited.

At any other time I might have been taken aback by something like this, but mindful that I was here to attend a special event put on in honour of a magician who, after years of study, meant to surprise his guests with an unusual performance, I wasn't even surprised when, having gone up the few steps and entered the hallway, I found myself in total darkness. I merely looked about me and, hearing a creak and a thunderous banging as the large door closed behind me, I assumed that this was all happening to magnify the effect.

I remained standing there, waiting to see what would come next.

However, a profound silence reigned and, at first, total darkness as well.

After the time it took my eyes, having passed from the moonlit night into darkness, to get used to the change, I noticed a lighter strip just a few paces ahead of me.

I went closer and saw that it was caused by the dim glint of the moon escaping through the chink in the door leading to an adjacent room.

I opened the door wide and entered the room. It was deserted and unfurnished, and although I hadn't been here for many years, I well remembered that this room had once acted as an antechamber through which to reach the corridor that led to the vast main room where larger festivities were usually held.

I also remembered that this was the way you went if you didn't want to enter by the front door, but, unobserved, through one of the side doors instead.

Knowing which way to go, I took the few steps towards the window through which that pale glimmer of the moon was coming in and found, next to it, the secret, wallpapered door to the corridor.

I had no problem feeling for the slight bump in the wall, shaped like the flat head of a little stud – a secret spring – and I duly pressed it, thereby opening the door as I had done countless times in the distant past.

Ahead of me I saw the long, vaulted corridor, but relieved of all decoration.

The dim glimmer of moonlight was struggling in through several windows, but it did afford just enough illumination to reveal clearly that the corridor was completely empty.

Where the moonlight did come in it bounced off the snow-white walls, and in part also off the smooth, square, black and white floor tiles, but in such a remarkable way that the reflection alone was enough to show when, high above the chateau, a little cloud had passed before the moon.

I entered the corridor.

But to my not inconsiderable surprise an odd cold washed over me, as if the corridor was open at the far end.

I didn't waste time pondering this, but carried on down the corridor until I reached the spot where it formed a right angle with another corridor.

This second corridor was also completely empty.

I went down it and, finding myself in yet a third corridor, I thought I'd reached the entrance to the hall. But where the door through which I'd passed unobserved numerous times in the past should have been, all I found was a bare wall.

So I went on to the corner, only to find that the third corridor met a fourth, likewise forming with it a right angle.

There could be no doubt that in the intervening years since I last visited the chateau there had been some changes of which I had no inkling.

At least the corridors had been reconstructed and the entrance to the hall had either been bricked up or relocated.

So I continued down the fourth corridor, but failed to find any door here either, or any way out.

It also struck me that the corridors that I had passed through formed a regular parallelogram.

Accordingly I passed from the fourth corridor back into the first.

From the reflection on the walls and floor I believed I was in the corridor that I had entered from the hallway. But the door through which I'd entered it and which had closed behind me in a baffling way wasn't to be found.

I spent several minutes scouring the walls, but my efforts were in vain.

Having puzzled briefly over how this was possible, I eventually inferred from the evidence that I was in corridors from which there was no escape unless my friend the magic merchant deigned to utter his spell-breaking *Ephpheta!*

I freely admit that this introduction to my friend's art had caught me unprepared.

To lure someone from his home at night under the pretext of going to a party, all the way to a chateau where he can readily detect the festivities going on, to let him enter through an open door and lure him into corridors from which no egress can be found – that struck me as a bit of wizardry as tricky as it was original.

"Let us bide out time, then, until the adept magician deigns to release us from our confinement," I thought and calmly went along the first corridor to the second, along the second to the third and on and on, finally returning to the spot from which I had set out.

Now and again I stopped and listened, but heard nothing except the occasional rustle of the wind as it passed over the chateau or thrust at the shutters, often making them rattle like a convict's chains.

In due course even these sounds died out for good and a dark, deathly hush settled about the corridors, broken only by the hollow, almost creepy echo of my footsteps.

At first I was quite calm, but after half an hour or so had passed, I grew somewhat impatient.

After almost an hour, as I still wandered aimlessly from corridor to corridor, I was acutely aware that my impatience was growing and growing.

I began traversing the corridors at a brisker pace, eventually becoming aware of starting to tire, and then I grew quite peevish.

I called out my friend's name several times, but my voice just bounced back from the arch of the next corridor, as if someone were laughing spitefully there in the distance.

By now almost running along the corridors, I warmed up somewhat, only to feel the cold even more acutely whenever I stopped or slowed.

There was nothing for it but to maintain an ever brisker pace...

I was growing ever more tired, but the cold drove me on and on...

My irritation and surliness grew in proportion to the protraction of my time in "prison".

Suddenly, however, the idea took hold in my soul that I was, after all, the victim of an illusion, that this was all a phantasmagoria inside my fevered brain.

I quickened my pace even more.

I literally ran the length of all four corridors, stopping again at the spot where – as I believed – the door by which I entered had been.

I searched for it briefly, but only briefly – the chill that was by now making all my limbs quiver and quake drove me back down the corridors...

I well recall how anxiety now took over in my soul. At first only a dull, indefinite sense of unease, which just grew and grew until it became full-fledged anxiety.

There was also my sense that the corridor ahead was growing narrower – I hurried forward..., but unimpeded, and as soon as I reached the next corridor it seemed this time as if its ceiling was lowering up ahead and the whole corridor narrowing...

By the time I grew fully aware of these particular optical illusions, I thought I must have been wandering the corridors for at least three hours… Every minute was becoming like a quarter of an hour.

I stamped my feet, clapped my hands, shouted myself hoarse – but all around me was the eerie silence, broken only by the sounds made by me.

Each time I stopped, a mysterious, chilling breath swept over me and drove me ever onwards…

I was running again… I could feel the blood seething in my veins, the sweat streaming from my brow and down my cheeks – but a mystical power kept driving me on…

All I could see ahead was the grey, seemingly narrowing corridor, and in the distance a total void gaped back at me, stirring in my soul something approaching terror…

By this stage I was barely aware whether this was all real – I had my doubts – but then the realisation came creeping back that I had seen with my own eyes the chateau all so radiant, that it couldn't have been a reflection, because the moon had already begun to sink westwards and I'd seen the eastern and northern parts of the house lit up. I recalled speaking to the porter, seeing the dark figures flitting about outside and hearing music before I went inside, in short it all had to be real…, and yet I couldn't grasp how it was possible that all I could hear now was the dull echo of my own footsteps and voice, as if I were lingering in the corridors of an uninhabited chateau…

And out of the jumble of strange ideas triggered by my predicament, suddenly one all-inclusive thought surfaced…

This is exactly what it must be like for anyone blundering through life from one illusion to the next, from one delusion to the next, vainly seeking something to hold on to, no matter how slight that might be – this is exactly what it must be like when the human brain fills with that enigmatic chaos of crisscrossing and contradictory thoughts and imaginings that precedes the fateful, frightful mental condition that we call lunacy...

This thought hit me quite suddenly and in a twinkling drove the blood towards my head.

An involuntary yelp escaped my breast. I staggered, my tired legs stopped running – I fell to the ground... My soul suffered a blackout...

But what's this?

Didn't I just hear a faint sound of music, and was that a clear strip of light that flashed before me?...

I rubbed my eyes and tried to stand. In a few seconds I succeeded...

I saw that I was standing in a vaulted corridor – a door before me was slightly ajar and through it were coming that strip of light and the sounds of music...

I staggered to the door.

Through the chink between the door and its frame I could see into a large, brightly lit room...

However, my eyes were still so bleary that I could barely make anything out, though I was clearly beginning to take things in. I wanted to take a few steps forward, but then staggered again and had to prop myself up against the corridor wall.

I SPENT ABOUT FIVE MINUTES in this pose, then slowly and cautiously I approached the door and opened it just a little so as to get an easier view of the room.

Only then was I completely convinced that I was standing at the door that I knew afforded unobserved access to the room and that the music had been coming from this brightly lit room in which a large number of guests were gathered.

Plainly I was not in the corridor of an empty, uninhabited chateau, I was not standing in one of the corridors from which there seemed to be no way out, but in a corridor and before a half-open door through which, many years previously, I had frequently passed without hindrance into the room and back out again.

So how had it come about that for three hours I'd wandered lost – as it had seemed – through the simplest labyrinth of four corridors that formed a regular parallelogram, how had it come about that for so long I'd been unable to find this way out of the labyrinth, when it now seemed so obvious? – I could find no explanation.

However, at that instant I didn't trouble myself greatly with trying to unravel the mystery; I was still in a state of considerable excitement and, moreover, I was teased by curiosity to know who was in the room and what was going to happen next.

Having removed my overcoat and tossed aside my hat, I slipped unobserved into the doorway and stood there rooted on the threshold, leaning against the doorframe.

The huge, high-ceilinged and gloriously bejewelled room was illuminated by so very many lights that, scouring the floor, you might easily have found even a single poppy seed.

A first glance about the room showed me that assembled here was indeed a large and distinguished company – but all male.

There could have been as many as two hundred people present. They were seated at tables set out in a semi-circle, but in such a way that you could walk round each one, and from each table there was a good view of the black curtain that hung from ceiling to floor, partitioning off a section of the room.

Numerous liveried servants scurried among the tables, waiting on the guests. Others kept dashing in and out of the room, bringing all manner of dishes and drinks on silver trays.

I couldn't detect where the orchestra was located, but I could clearly hear the delicate tones of some melancholy tune. So there could be no doubt that there was an orchestra, either hidden from view or in one of the rooms adjacent.

The room was alive with activity and background noise, but all very subdued; I could hear the whispered conversations of the guests and the muffled calls of the waiters, but for me it all merged into an impenetrable whirr, as when the sound of a distant waterfall disturbs the silence of a forest.

At first, as I had foreseen, no one noticed me, which enabled me, therefore, to observe the entire company at will and in detail.

At the time I hardly knew any of the leading lights of Prague, marked out by their status or family background or attracting the attention of the widest circles through some other consideration – though some I did know by name, and to judge by the ones I did know and now recognised, this was a highly select gathering.

Recalling that the banquet had been organised by my friend's father at the behest of the Kinskys and that the family had invited most of the guests themselves, I wasn't surprised to see several members of the aristocracy at this table or that. I recognised one of the Lobkowitz princes, two Wallensteins, the son of the Prince of Windisch-Grätz, one of the Counts of Thurn and Taxis, two Kounitzes, the frail old Count Hanusch Kolowrat, the youngest of the Lichtensteins and two Rohans – almost all of them aristocrats who had been, all those years previously, regular guests of the Princes Kinsky.

All these, and some I didn't know, were sitting at one end of the semi-circle formed by the tables.

Nor was I surprised to recognise, at two tables at the opposite end of the semi-circle, the Archbishop of Prague, Prince Schwarzenberg, then two canons, the abbot of Strahov monastery, the generals of the Order of Knights of the Cross with the Red Star and of the Knights Hospitaller, the Provost of Vyšehrad and other church dignitaries, and at the next table the parish priests from St Nicholas' and Smíchov and several other clergymen unknown to me.

Next to the tables where the aristocracy was seated I saw two or three tables at which sat the provincial governor, the provincial commander of the imperial army, several generals and various higher- and lower-ranking officers, the Burgomaster of Prague, the Chief of Police, several Czech and German members of parliament, several gubernatorial and municipal counsellors and officials, as I judged them to be, of many different categories.

With them there were yet other guests who I was unable to identify.

They were mostly interesting characters and I was fairly certain that they could be categorised as scholars, university professors and the like. I did, in fact, recognise among them some of my erstwhile teachers from the Prague Polytechnic.

At the time I knew but few major literary figures, but I did recognise among the guests Pflegr, who was related to my friend, and Neruda, who had once been my and my friend's Czech teacher. They were both sitting at one of the centre tables and appeared to be engaged in a lively discussion.

My and my friend's friends, the ones who hadn't shown up at the tavern to which I'd invited them, were also present, seated at the table next to that of the literary gentlemen.

I might well have recognised many more outstanding personalities among the assembled throng, but my attention was distracted.

As one of the waiters flashed past me, he looked up at me and stopped. I recognised an old friend from the times when I was an almost daily visitor to the park and house.

"Ah, at last!" he said in a low voice, and his grey, deep-set eyes flared with a particular shine. "I must report at once that you're arrived... Do go down into the room and take your seat at the middle table."

He pointed to the table occupied by my and my friend's friends.

"Why there exactly?" I asked.

"Because it has been so ordered," said the poor fellow, who'd spent a lifetime obeying orders.

"But why?..."

"I don't know, nor do I need to know... but that's how it has to be... Just look how the guests are arranged. There's the nobility, opposite them the clergy, next to the aristocrats, bureaucrats and so on. 'Birds of a feather' has had to be our watchword... And so each in their particular groups you have doctors, lawyers, philosophers, architects, engineers, sculptors, actors, opera singers, painters, musicians, writers and so on, and those with no affiliation are also all together."

"But why? There never used to be any such rigmarole!" I observed.

"True, there wasn't, but today it's all very strict," he replied. "So, please...," he added in the funereal tone that only a nobleman's manservant can command, enjoining without recourse to words.

Then he pointed once more to the table at which my friends were seated.

"All right – I'll take my place as you have indicated, not wishing to cause you any unpleasantness," I said, mollified, and a few paces brought me right to my friends' table, while the waiter shot across the room and disappeared through the main entrance.

Hardly any of the guests noticed me.

Some did turn their heads, others stared, but not having seen me enter by the main door, they probably thought I'd left the table briefly and was now coming back. Some of my friends shook my hand, others welcomed me with a smile or a nod.

But before I sat down or said a word to any of my friends, the previously delicate, mournful music suddenly changed into a deafening fanfare.

A few moments later, the music fell silent, most of the lights in the room suddenly went out and as the black curtain hanging from ceiling to floor just a few paces behind us slowly parted, a resonant voice rang out into the silence that had ensued.

"The show begins!"

With the curtain now drawn aside completely, I saw a dais covered in black cloth, on it a low catafalque, only about two feet from the floor, and on the catafalque a metal coffin covered with a lid.

In the background and along the sides of the coffin were masses of beautiful, rare, exotic flowers. Tall church candles atop slender tapered spikes burned along both sides of the coffin.

At the head end of the coffin there was a huge laurel wreath, further down an officer's shako and sabre, and at the foot end a simple epitaph was to be seen:

BEDŘICH WÜNSCHER

K. u. K. Oberleutnant

Born 7 July 1841

Died 7 July 1866

The surprise was universal. The room fell so silent that even the slightest rustle could have been heard. And before long, through the silence came, as if originating from one of the side rooms, the sound of plaintive, mournful voices singing *Salve Regina*.

For as long as the singing continued no one uttered a word, and afterwards, when it subsided to be replaced by the deathly hush again, no one even stirred. Apart from me, there was probably no one in the room aware that all this was no more than an original piece of jiggery-pokery.

After quite a pause, the archbishop rose to his feet – he was probably the most impatient...

At the same instant, the coffin lid shot up into the air with a bang and remained hanging in the air between ceiling and floor the way, as it is claimed, the lid floats above the coffin of Mohammed.

In the open coffin I saw a corpse clad in the apparel of an army officer. However, I was too far away for a clear view of the facial features.

The room was still in total silence.

It was some minutes before one of the guests rose from the table reserved for doctors and professors from the faculty of Medicine. I recognised the unmistakable head of the Smíchov medical man, Dr Sperlich.

"The corpse must be examined!" he said and strode rapidly across to the coffin.

His colleagues followed him.

After these, the guests at the table for engineers and architects rose, followed by others; the philosophers and clergymen were the last.

In moments the catafalque was surrounded by almost all the guests. Closest to it stood some of the doctors, the rest holding back at a respectable distance, so it wasn't too hard to get up close to the coffin.

So I did, and standing at the corpse's head, I gazed into its immobile, pallid face...

It was the same face that I'd seen in Nechanitz, after the Battle of Sadowa...

The similarity to my friend's face was so extraordinary that, having gazed for some while upon those immobile features,

I simply couldn't believe that it wasn't my friend's corpse lying there before me.

Dr Sperlich ran his hand across the corpse's forehead, tried its pulse, unbuttoned the white doublet and, having opened the shirt at the chest, stated that what lay in the coffin was a genuine corpse – and embalmed.

Some of those who were standing closest followed his example in order to convince themselves of the truth of the doctor's assertion, and not one of them was in any doubt.

I, too, placed a hand on the forehead – it was cold as ice... I bent closer towards the face and detected not the slightest hint of breathing. The hand was also ice-cold and the half-bared chest showed unmistakable signs of death...

Dr Sperlich, desirous of proving beyond all doubt that they were standing before a body devoid of feeling, took out his penknife, open it and stuck it into the corpse's chest... The corpse only stirred with the blow, remaining otherwise without change...

Some of the guests, quite incapable of accounting for all this, exchanged various views; others began returning to their seats...

After five or six minutes had elapsed, there were only about twenty left by the coffin.

Before likewise returning to my place I took one last close look into the corpse's face...

There was a pink petal of some exotic bloom on his lips and just as I had focussed on his face, it moved, as if wafted by feeble breathing...

I looked even more attentively into the face and noticed the eyelashes seeming to quiver and shortly after that the chest to swell somewhat...

I quickly reached for the corpse's hand to check whether my eyes weren't deceiving me... The hand was no longer ice-cold, but warm to the touch, and so far as I could tell its temperature was rising quite fast.

I was thinking about bringing this remarkable change to the notice of Dr Sperlich, who was still close at hand, but before I'd quite made up my mind, I saw the corpse's eyelids slowly open and close...

I couldn't suppress an involuntary yelp.

Some of those standing closest stepped even closer, but then they almost all stepped back in haste and utter amazement...

The corpse had stirred, or rather quivered, as if an electric current had suddenly passed through it... And I observed quite clearly the symptoms of animal life returning.

In about three minutes the corpse moved its head, then both hands and seconds later its whole body.

Having hauled itself up with considerable effort, the corpse remained in that position for several moments – then it flopped back into the coffin – then it hauled itself up again and remained in a sitting position.

The bewilderment of those present changed into frank amazement. Whatever the effect of the unexpected scene on this or that guest, it seemed absolutely certain that there was no one present who wasn't astonished to the maximum degree.

Everyone seemed to have been expecting a fairly ordinary magic show and hadn't expected it to begin in such an extravagantly original manner.

With the corpse sitting erect inside the coffin the room briefly slipped back into silence.

No one scarcely so much as stirred. The eyes of all were fixed on the remarkable automaton which but a moment ago various experts had been conclusively convinced was an embalmed corpse.

And now the corpse was showing signs of life! It sat there motionless for a time, but its eyes were shining...

After a moment the corpse moved its head, as if surveying those present in search of someone in particular, then it nodded as if satisfied – a faint smile briefly lit up its face, its lips parted and it spoke: *"De mortuis nil nisi bene!"*

And how amazing! Everything that had so far been played out before the guests' eyes had failed to raise in any one of them a single word of admiration or surprise – it took the sound of a human voice to evoke a response and the room erupted in applause to cries of "Bravo! Brilliant!"

Simultaneously with this uproar all the lights suddenly went out, leaving the room in total darkness.

A few seconds later the lights came back on and there before our eyes was not a catafalque, coffin and an enlivened corpse, but a simple table, next to it a chair and behind it my friend in elegant, black drawing-room attire.

Again the room resounded to a storm of sustained applause and cries from every side of "Brilliant!" and "Bravo!"

After the storm of acclaim subsided, my friend addressed those present thus:

"Gentlemen, I apologise for opening my show in such an unusual manner, but as I began, so I mean to end. However, permit to fill the interlude with a few words that many of you may find interesting. What you see before you is a man not with his own brain, but with another's..."

Whereupon he reached for his head with his right hand and easily, like a cap, he removed the top part of his skull, holding which in his hand, he took a few steps forward.

"Almost everything that I'm about to say is going to seem improbable," my friend eventually began. "But if any of you learned gentlemen wishes to check for himself, do please feel free – So!"

My friend stepped down and headed for the centre of the semi-circle, where he sat down on a vacant chair and added:

"Any of you with expertise in anatomy and physiology is welcome to examine my brain!"

Several guests seated at the professorial tables rose, surrounded my friend and began their examination. One then began the commentary:

"It's true! What we see here is a genuine skull with a piece peeled off and the surface of the brain. The surface exhibits perfectly normal convolutions. Under the microscope some might exhibit deviant shapes or sizes, but as it stands, there is nothing observable that isn't entirely normal.

"Likewise the familiar grey matter composed of nerve cells and dispersed in convolutions over the whole surface of the brain is clearly visible – and for the benefit of the layman I would add that modern physiology indicates this matter as the seat of the awareness, of thoughts, aptitudes and memories. More than that I cannot say."

"So I'll say something instead," my friend put in. He stood up, restored the skull and strolled casually over to his table.

"The brain just examined by one of your august number," my friend commenced his preliminary account, "is not, as I have said, my own, but someone else's. I borrowed it for the same purpose for which billions of people have borrowed, since time immemorial, the most precious products of the activity of other people's brains – their ideas...

"It is, I maintain, easier to think with someone else's brain, boast of someone else's idea and make oneself and others happy than to spark an idea of one's own out of one's own brain...

"I thought long and hard about the brain I would hold best suited to my end and eventually decided on the brain of a man held by the entire educated world to be one of the sharpest thinkers.

"I knew that the man's brain was kept in a certain museum in England; by subterfuge and guile I managed to possess myself of this most precious treasure, and when the chance came, following the Battle of Sadowa, the top of my skull having been sliced off, I replaced my own brain with Newton's."

"Impossible!" rang out from the table of doctors, anatomists and physiologists.

"Downright silly!" came from the philosophers' table.

"Utter blasphemy!" from the theologians'.

My friend was unmoved by this multilateral exhibition of disapproval. I'd say he'd been expecting it, so, quite unruffled, he went on:

"Please, gentlemen, forgive me. Each of us thinks in his own way, each conceives of, defines and gives names to various concepts and objects in the manner in which he has been taught, the manner to which he is accustomed, the manner that has taken his fancy. Whatever the consideration behind how he names things, nothing changes – they remain just as they truly are..."

By this twist of sophistry my friend clearly went some way towards quelling the indignation of the majority of the guests, but he convinced no one.

It was therefore unsurprising when a cry sprang from the middle of the throng:

"Proof – we want irrefutable proof!"

"For the moment," my friend began again, "I can't give you irrefutable proof, any more than any of us can irrefutably prove the most brilliant hypothesis of all time, Newton's universal gravitation...

"So, for the time being, please try, gentlemen, to accept my position in the manner favoured by all who, careless of any evidence, invariably rely on what is known as personal conviction...

"Please be convinced of the truth of what I have said at least as much as the ancient Greeks were convinced of the divinity of their Zeus and the Romans their Jupiter..., as the ancient Jews were convinced of the divinity of their gloomy Jehovah and as the orthodox Jews of today remain convinced as to the Second Coming..."

"Excellent!" rang out from the theologians' table.

Ignoring the interruption, my friend went on:

"... as the ancient Indians were convinced of the omnipotence of their progenitor of the world, Brahma..., as they were convinced of the immortality of the soul, which transmigrates from one body to another and, thus purified, returns to the eternal primal being from which it had sprung..., as later Indians were convinced that besides Brahma the gods Siva and Vishnu are also eternal, omniscient and omnipotent..., as they were convinced of the truth of the ingenious, uplifting and poetical idea underlying their religion that good shall strive against evil until such time as evil shall be brought low and obliterated forever..."

"Excellent! Excellent!" rang out from the theologians' table once more.

"... and as we – that is, we who, as babes and not of our own volition, entered the Christian communion – are all convinced that, unless it were the will of our almighty, all-knowing, supremely wise, kind, just, indulgent and merciful God, not even a hair of our heads will perish, and yet that any of us, having committed a mortal sin, may expect eternal damnation..."

These words were followed by a stony silence from the theologians' table, though some muted approval did come from that of the philosophers.

"Let us concede for now, gentlemen," my friend went on, "that my brain has indeed been replaced by Newton's...

"How bizarre, how puny must our allegedly enlightened age seem to me!

"We research past ages and smile understandingly, or even mockingly, at the sublime naivety, crudeness and ineptitude of our forefathers without it ever crossing our minds that future ages will take the same mocking view of ours...

"We swell with pride that our age is an age of enlightenment and progress – while millions of our brethren dwell in brutish obtuseness...

"We are jubilant that the principle of humanity, unknown throughout the ages, has finally won recognition, while in utterly selfish indifference we look on at the pain and penury of the thousands who, having been born, eke out a miserable existence only to die to no purpose... Where would a penetrating, ruthless mind place us, now, at the end of the nineteenth century, if it were to analyse our endeavours and objectives? – At the stage of drafting formulae, in an age of definitions – in a century of empty phrases...

"The attainments of the human intellect may be quite familiar to many of us, but for a thousand reasons born of disgusting egoism we avoid them, lest we run up against prejudices...

"Can it be called progress when all manner of fallacies are still called for, though not for the purposes of salvation – for there is no salvation in fallacy – but for the enslavement of mankind?..."

"Oh, do cut the moralising!" came from the tables of theologians, philosophers and bureaucrats simultaneously.

"No, no, do go on, go on!" – thus the call from the tables of artists, writers, lawyers and doctors.

"I maintain that any of us would concede," my friend pursued his deliberation, "that the human brain has always been made of the same matter, that it has always consisted of the same parts, that its performance has always been governed by the same rules, that its surface has consisted of the same convolutions and that within those convolutions, dispersed over the entire surface and stored inside the brain in two large ganglions there has always been, since time immemorial, the same wondrous grey matter – swathed in a white material and consisting of nerve cells – where modern physiology locates thought, the intellect, our discernment and our aptitudes...

"So the overriding organ of thought and competence is the same – but what are its achievements?

"Why do they differ so substantially from the achievements of that same organ in ages past? What is the reason for the brains of our own times not producing ideas like those born in the brains of Homer, Sophocles, Aeschylus, Euripides, Aristophanes, Shakespeare, Cervantes, Dante, Milton, Petrarch, Tasso, Calderón, Molière, Voltaire, Rousseau and others?

"Where today are the brains that produced such wondrous works as bequeathed to us by Michelangelo, Raphael, Rubens, Titian, Murillo, van Dyck, Rembrandt, Guido Reni, Leonardo da Vinci, Hogarth, Salvator Rosa, Correggio, Annibale Carracci, Ostade, Ruysdael, and even our own Škréta and Brandl? Where in our own day can we find brains to match the long line of brilliant sculptors going back to Phidias, Scopas and Praxiteles?

"Where are the brains from which magnificent cathedrals, palaces, pantheons and other structures sprang?

"Where are the brains of Mozart, Beethoven, Haydn? Where the brains of Garrick, Kean, Talma, Rachelek and others... And yet we live in an age of what? Progress! Where does this progress show?"

"In modern pedagogy," a voice filled with irony suddenly piped up from the lawyers' tables.

"That's right," my friend added. "Modern pedagogy may indeed boast of some extraordinary successes. Our watchword is study and its object is the accumulation of knowledge. And from our tenderest age we are whipped roundly and with unparalleled zeal, both morally and literally, into making our brains work harder and in unusual, not to say extraordinary, ways...

"And yet the amazing grey matter of our brain, which, as they say, is the wellspring of our aptitudes, can basically never be any different from how it actually is, any more than the outcome of its mysterious processes can ever be any other than as it has been conditioned by this organ of thinking, feeling and recollecting..."

"While jurisprudence...," came mockingly from the pedagogues' table.

"... may indeed boast of a most excellent achievement," my friend interrupted it. "Since for all its endeavours it has so far failed to define even the *very concept* of right...

"Though it *has* blessed mankind with billions of laws, some quite trifling – obscure laws and plain, but always elastic... And any one of these laws can be interpreted in a thousand and one different ways, any one of them can be sidestepped and any one of them can be countered...

"And how odd is this ...! It takes bayonets and artillery to protect even modern justice... and in the background the prison gate still yawns and punishment looms...

"And who, pray, can boast of knowing all those countless laws?... Billions of poor folk wander and grope about in the dark... We all know that at every step we might trip and find ourselves in the ambuscade of a law of which we have no ken... And if it were not for pure instinct..."

"Excellent!" came mischievously from a table of doctors.

"I note with interest," my friend continued, "that our doctor friends, who may be deemed, with total justification, to be mankind's greatest benefactors, recognise the merits of their lawyer colleagues.

"But who of their number can step forward and say: I do not act like the wise Eristratos, of whom it has been written somewhere that while he was obliging to patricians and would pour himself luscious glasses of raspberry juice to afford himself relief, when it came to common folk who'd turned a bit yellow, he would slit open their bellies without ado, probe their liver, probe their spleen, sprinkle in some remedial powder, close the gash and surrender his charges to... the will of God?"

This allusion was rewarded with thunderous applause accompanied by cries of "Brilliant!" from every side.

After a pause, my friend went on:

"And yet it has to be acknowledged that it was indeed doctors who did their level best to apply their science to the relief of human suffering. Surgery has seen untold progress...

"Yet the final outcome? Let us concede that the medical sciences really will achieve perfection, that every injury will be made good, every disease cured. But what will be the consequence?

"Very simple – very, very simple... People will no longer die prematurely of induced or accidental maladies as hitherto, but will live for fifty, seventy even a hundred years in what? In the marasmus of senility. And they'll still die anyway...

"My point being that no matter what high degrees of perfection the medical arts were to rise to, they would never achieve more than putting mortality off by a generation or two... That's all! So much for that huge investment of intellectual endeavour!...

"'But what does it matter if we return twenty, thirty or fifty years sooner or later to the place whence we came? As long as our brain's mysterious grey matter is in its normal state – of course, many of us may be frightened, even terrified at the prospect...

"But the billions of beings who have gone before us are the guarantee that, like them, we shall pass, that no human power can ward off our final destiny..."

"Yet how many works of art or science might have been brought to perfection if their authors hadn't died prematurely!" someone at the writers' table shouted.

"True," my friend continued. "But only for it to come into being, be perfected, and then go the way of all earthly things – ultimately disintegrating into nought...

"The most enthralling performance by an actor or orator is gone in an instant and is generally forgotten within a generation or two. The most solid, most magnificent buildings and memorials descend to dust after millennia..., fate often catches up with the most beautiful paintings and statues after mere centuries... Whatever we undertake, everything is doomed ineluctably to total destruction..."

Following these words the archbishop rose to his feet, and turning half-way to face both my friend and the assembled guests, spoke in his amiable, resonant voice:

"Begging your forgiveness for this interruption: I do not know what our artist's words are leading up to, so I would not wish to utter any rebuke. However, we of the clergy have had to listen here to words that are, not to put too fine a point on it, contentious.

"They may have been uttered in the guise of sarcasm or humour, and they appear to be underpinned by science; but their core is incompatible with our own views. Therefore, if the gentleman means to continue with his account, which appears to be vital to his future experiments, I beg him to avoid issues that it is not within the powers of man to resolve."

The archbishop resumed his seat, but his words appeared not to have had the impact on the audience that he had sought.

The eyes of all those present were fixed on my friend, who had stood there by his table, listening to the archbishop with stoical resignation before replying with the same affability and courtesy with which he had been addressed.

"I likewise beg your forgiveness as I depart from my narrative in order to respond. I wish to assure His Eminence that it has not been, and is not, my intention to concern myself with, or seek to resolve any mysteries attaching to, religion, and this has certainly not arisen from my not having thus far touched on philosophy, the scholarly antithesis of religion.

"The point I am seeking to make will become clear once my final demonstration is concluded. So for this reason I crave your indulgence..."

"Excellent!" rang out from several sides at once.

"Do continue!" came from the artists' and scholars' tables simultaneously, and my friend took up from where he had left off:

"We pride ourselves on our progress in science and we forget that all that science has achieved is put to both good and bad purposes.

"Printing – claimed to be mankind's greatest blessing – is exploited equally by the tyrant and the humanitarian, the clever man and the buffoon, the religious fanatic and the most sober thinker, the honest, conscientious scholar and the shameless charlatan; printing has served and will continue to serve equally the noblest and the basest causes...

"So in what way does man's much-vaunted blessing manifest itself? Where is the guarantee that this remarkable idea-disseminating invention will ultimately reside exclusively in the hands of honest men and serve only for good?"

"It surely doesn't take Newton's brain to come up with such a banal question as that!" someone at the writers' table added out loud.

"Excellent!" came simultaneously from the military officers' table. "Since time immemorial pen pushers have been the most useless creatures in the world!"

"True," my friend continued after a brief pause, "Newton's brain existed only once, and having fulfilled its purpose, it can never re-appear in the same guise. But the mysterious grey matter of the human brain, which our physiologists deem to be the wellspring of thought and the seat of our intellectual capacity, does remain essentially the same...

"Thoughts arise from it and man's faculties are concealed within it... And yet for all the diversity of ideas and aptitudes there remain those unknown laws by which this mysterious process is governed, ever the same; in a word, there is but one logic and that is eternal...

"Who knows if the brain of some peasant, servant or slave – now long gone and forgotten – if it had come into being under the same circumstances and if it had worked in the same direction and in the same, or perhaps merely similar conditions as Newton's brain, who knows if that brain might not have arrived, and sooner, at the same scholarly outcomes as Newton's? Who knows if it might not have arrived at even more ingenious conclusions?"

"With so many ifs to it, that's a sentence that would be hard to counter," said another unknown voice coming from the writers' table.

"So what use is the ridiculous cult of so-called great minds," my friend continued, "since we know that the same conditions under which this or that celebrated act or performance came about have existed, or exist, in thousands of others who happen not to have pursued the same outcome..."

"Bravo! Bravo!" came from the table of the nobility.

"And what use is the even more ridiculous cult of those – I would call them mindless – minds, whose acclaim is down to the minds – hired and paid for – of others..."

A muted mumbling of dissent could be heard coming from the tables of the aristocrats and bureaucrats, but my friend ploughed on:

"What is the point of idolising our own spirit, our own acts, our own age? What is served by endless paeans to the age of enlightenment and progress, when we still have so far to go before we reach genuine universal enlightenment?... When we know that almost all that the human mind has achieved in all ages remains liable to abuse?...

"Isn't the modern worker operating some machine still the same slave that he ever was? Is his life any more pleasant, more secure, more filled with joy than before?

"Don't we all know that *all* the sciences, from their queen, mathematics, right down to the least, often phony pseudo-science, exploit their earlier, as well as their more recent attainments also for the mutual destruction of mankind?

"Developments in modern strategy and tactics are evidence that all new means of communication are used to enable vast armies to reach, as fast as possible, the place where they can most easily wipe each other out.

"Mathematics, chemistry, optics, mechanics and the entire gamut of other sciences tender all their latest and best achievements to this end. Even venerable history, which only describes facts, and tried and tested pedagogy, which signals models to follow, often serve the same purpose.

"In what way, pray, are all those heroes of whom historians have kept us mindful exemplary? To what end are all those modern manifestos, army orders and all the major and minor devices, often construed with great sophistication, that are used to fire human souls to fervent, furious and often futile combat?"

"Stop denigrating your own kind!" came from the officers' table, and from somewhere at the back a gloomy, but resonant voice piped up:

"What's all this got to do with your magic demonstration?"

"That's simple," my friend retorted. "My experiment is based on a scientific hypothesis..."

"So get on with it then!" cried the same unknown voice.

"No, stay with your explanation!" came from the tables on the right.

"No, no, the demonstration. The demonstration!" shouted from the left.

"Speak! Speak!" called out from the centre.

The room filled with such a cacophony that soon nothing being said was remotely intelligible.

The cacophony lasted for several minutes and, just as a matter of interest, I would point out that the tables occupied by guests accustomed to public speaking, such as churchmen, members of parliament and professors, exhibited the greatest impatience and called for the demonstration, whereas the tables at which sat guests rarely given to explaining anything, such as artists, engineers, architects, soldiers etc., were strikingly in favour of my friend's exhilarated discourse.

He was therefore obliged to indulge, for now, both sides.

"Your honourable throng has split into two main camps," he began, the noise having subsided somewhat. "As a poor artist craving the recognition of all who have a sense for my art I cannot as yet oblige one side over the other, because I don't know which side is actually more receptive to my performance. Accordingly, I have no option but to indulge both sides at once – so I beg to be permitted to complete my account, after which I will make the demonstration without further ado."

"Agreed!" came the cry from right, left and centre all at once, whereupon my friend went on:

"Modern man's proud boasts about how progressive the age in which he lives is are truly to be deplored. For it appears that a momentary, frequently problematical success on the part of some gifted individual has the effect of blinding thousands of others with the unfounded assumption that it amounts to some amazing advance...

"And yet man's pretentiousness shines through with ever greater intensity. The 'lord and king of creation', whose spirit will allegedly force Nature to bow down before him..., this arrogant, proud, conceited giant of creation is shown up in the light of strict science and logic as a, frankly, pitiable dwarf...

"Even in our earliest childhood our teachers sought to teach us that human sight is weaker than the eagle's or falcon's, man's hearing, smell and other senses duller than those of many other creatures...

"Man has always known this, hence the ghastly pursuit of means by which to sharpen the senses... So his sharpening of them has been artificial; thus he has invariably grown ever more acutely aware of what a pitiable, wretched, miserable little creature he is...

"He took an autopsy knife and dissected his own body... He found and sorted his organs, tried to see how they worked and what they were for, determined how important, vital they were, and arrived at the conviction that life 'after the divine image of the created lord of creation' hardly differed from the life of the most inferior creatures...

"He recorded the workings of the mind... He made great progress, but failed to define accurately the boundary between good and evil... He has penetrated the depths of the earth and has gone even deeper into the cosmos with his physical and mental vision... He has tried to establish the laws of the universe, but by none of this has he succeeded in keeping at bay that awful awareness of the inevitability of death and oblivion...

"To come into being, live, suffer – then perish, disintegrate into basic elements and vanish forever...

"That is the frightening prospect that scientific progress lays bare before man's eyes...

"Pretending not to know, seeking solace in illusions and utopias, is no use whatsoever and smacks of cowardice... Let us be aware of how far we have come...

"But what are we to think of human life with regard to this greatest achievement of the intellect? Do we value human life as it deserves to be valued?... Who among us can step up and prove that he has destroyed a single life and that that life has re-emerged since?... And yet all the terrible mutual slaughter that still goes on – whether swift through violence, or gradual through gruelling endeavour and suffering!..."

My friend fell silent, as if needing to pause for breath.

Not a rustle disturbed the deathly hush that now reigned.

The speaker clearly seemed to be stifling his thoughts rather than giving them free rein, hence the favourable impression his ecstatic discourse had been making.

After a short pause, my friend continued:

"And so neither I, nor anyone else, could restore life to a dead body... My entire art is based on speed and in all matters I rely on the sluggishness of thought processes.

"It is widely held that nothing is faster that thought. This view is wrong. Those cold, inexorable, but also utterly sincere friends of good sense – numbers – have latterly proved the opposite: it has been ascertained and calculated that by comparison with the speed of light and electricity, the speed of thought is amazingly insignificant...

"If I touch the skin on someone's leg, the impression takes as much as one-third of a second to pass through the spinal cord to the brain as the central organ of our awareness, whereas the same interval is enough for light to travel over fourteen thousand miles, and electricity, conducted by a copper wire, almost thirty-one thousand miles.

"And that same dilly-dallying – the time required for the impression of touching to travel along the spinal cord – apparently affects all impressions passing through the brain..."

My friend again fell briefly silent.

I have to confess that in that moment I hadn't the slightest idea of the nature of the demonstration that he was contemplating.

His piecemeal delivery was teasing my curiosity and I mentally allied myself to those who demanded it be executed without delay. However, despite that, and not wishing to cause my friend even the slightest hindrance, I continued to keep my counsel even as he picked up where he had left off.

"Modern man is apt to hold forth as grandly on immortality as he is on the speed of thought, progress and other such, while he knows full well that the final, inescapable end is what? Oblivion... He has striven, and still strives for all he is worth to conserve an image of man as a scene set out before his descendants; but none of his artistry, of any kind, has ever succeeded in preserving more than a shadow of that image – a shadow that fades with the passage of time and begins to disappear and break up into its basic elements, finally to vanish completely and forever, just like the original.

"I have been thinking about this for several years, and my art, reliant on all the achievements of science to which I have had access, can now conjure up any long-lost image or scene even after a hundred years, nay millennia, before the human gaze..."

"How so? How so?" came the cry from various directions at once, interrupting my friend.

The curiosity that he had evidently wished to stir up now prevailed. But he, as if he hadn't heard it, went on:

"If someone, before the invention of glass, telescopes and microscopes and in the presence of such an august company of his contemporaries as I find myself before now, had claimed that it would become possible one day, by means of certain instruments, to see to a distance of many miles, and that it would be possible to examine closely even heavenly bodies, the greatest mind of the time would doubtless mistrust the claim it was hearing.

"The same thing would have happened if, before the invention of steam engines, telegraphy and suchlike, someone had claimed that a journey could be made in several hours that at the time needed several months, or that it was possible to reach an arrangement with someone a hundred miles away in the twinkling of an eye.

"Today we would merely smile benevolently at disbelief at any such possible impossibility, but, that notwithstanding, I am sure that until I have carried out my demonstration, I shall also not be granted credence if I make so bold as to assert anything of the kind.

"The thing is, I have succeeded in inventing a substance from which it is possible to create a device that looks to all intents and purposes like an ordinary pair of spectacles, but faced with which even the very finest microscopes and telescopes available can go hang their heads. These spectacles enable one to see with absolute clarity an image at any distance, however remote, say a billion miles…"

"Impossible! – Balderdash!" came from various directions.

"Bearing in mind what I said before," my friend continued, "I also have had to expect not to be believed, any more than I would have been believed over five hundred years ago, had I maintained – as is now proven beyond dispute – that the Earth goes round the Sun and not vice versa.

"For that reason I am not remotely surprised that your honourable selves are pleased to call impossible and balderdash what I said before about inventing a substance and device to outshine all the finest contemporary telescopes, yet too simple for the human mind to envision. But that is not all: I have succeeded in inventing something apparently even more improbable than the foregoing.

"It is not an invention in the true sense of the word, because it has been known since prehistory, but its application is truly modern...

"Anyone will be surprised at its simplicity, but anyone who knows that the results of all human thought can be captured in very few words, anyone who knows that the apparent chaos of the universe, all the myriad of disparate forces of nature, is governed by a single law, will at least concede that the resultant of only a handful of these forces can be used to a particular purpose...

"I have succeeded in inventing, or, rather, putting to good use, a most precious kind of driver, known since prehistoric times, a driver that outstrips the speed of light, even surpassing the force of nature hitherto deemed the fastest – electricity..."

"Utopia!" echoed once again from various directions at once.

"And yet in due course I shall prove the very opposite," my friend continued, "and not just the force, but also the device that enables the effect of that remarkable force to be investigated and used for the boldest experiments and demonstrations..., it was designed and made by me and it is available here to be used at will by anyone who cares to convince himself of the truth of my words."

T HEN HE RAISED HIS HEAD and cast a glance upwards.

It was then that I first noticed that at the spot where previously the metal coffin lid had floated between floor and ceiling there now hung, motionless, a great regular triangle. One angle pointed straight to the ceiling, its opposite side being horizontal.

The triangle was quite large enough for two people to stand comfortably within it. I couldn't tell what it was made of. It seemed to be made of strong, shiny wire; at least, all three of its sides gleamed as if rays from the lights in the room were being reflected off the wire's smooth surface.

However, before I had time to take a good look at the odd device from a distance, my friend gave a simple wave of his hand and instantly the triangle flew down and remained standing on the table in front of my friend.

And how very strange! It was only now that I registered the two shiny objects hanging from the two bottom angles; when the triangle had been dangling in the air a moment before I hadn't spotted them.

My friend reached for the objects with both hands at the same time, placed them on the table and said: "Anyone wishing to see for themselves may come up and examine my appliances."

The guests surged towards the table from all sides.

I, too, now uncommonly curious, hurried over towards my friend and with considerable effort got close in to his table so that I might examine the devices at ease.

What I saw on the table looked like two ordinary pairs of spectacles. I picked up one of them so as to look through the lens and see if it differed from ordinary ones, but I have to confess that I could discern nothing aberrant or unusual. It looked like perfectly ordinary, uncut glass.

The other device was odder. What had looked from a distance like stout, shiny wire was an ever so thin, unknown, shiny material, gossamer-like, but as stiff and unyielding as wire. Its similarity to stout wire as I'd seen it from a distance had been, then, an optical illusion.

Not only I, but also some of the other guests, satisfied ourselves on the matter with our own eyes and hands.

After a few minutes, my friend, in the most courteous way possible, appealed to the curious guests to return to their seats, and once they had, he resumed his speech.

"First and foremost," he said, "I have to say something on the basic facts known about the speed of light, which is going to be vital to a readier understanding of the speed of my instrument. The speed of light is known to be estimated at over forty-two thousand miles per second.

"So a ray of light reaches us from the Moon in roughly a second and a half, and from the Sun in around eight minutes. The light of Jupiter needs about half an hour to reach Earth, Saturn's about an hour, from Uranus it's two and from Neptune, the furthermost planet known, roughly three hours...

"The fixed star closest to Earth, that is, the most luminous of the stars of magnitude 1, is around four billion miles away. Thus its light takes no less than three thousand two hundred years to reach us.

"Fixed stars of magnitude 12 are, as Struve has calculated, five billion miles away and their light takes about four thousand years to reach us.

"The distance of nebulae from Earth was estimated by Herschel at thirty-two thousand billion miles; here the light therefore needs twenty-four thousand years to reach us.

"However, Herschel and Maedler believed that the stars that form the many planetary nebulae are three hundred thousand times further away from us than fixed stars of magnitude 1; and then Rosse's giant telescope has revealed stars so remote that their light takes around three million years to reach us...

"From this it follows that the so-called universe must be at least thirty million years old, that's to say at least as old as the time it takes for the light from these stars to reach us...

"But these are all things familiar to anyone with an education and I only mention them as evidence in support of my claim.

"Since it is possible to see across such distances by means of polished lenses, why then would it not be possible to see things by means of a device of incomparably greater precision – the case of my invention, seeing here on Earth, a star of, say, magnitude 12 as clearly as the unimpaired human eye can see, unaided, tiny objects from a distance of ten to twelve inches?"

"Sheer humbug!" a grumpy voice let itself be heard from somewhere at the back.

A hint of a smile flitted across my friend's face, like the smile of one who is sure of victory.

"Until I give you proof that what I am saying is true," he went on, "anything that I have said may be called into question. However, anyone must concede that should one of us be able to make the roughly five-billion-mile trip from some star of magnitude 12 to here on Earth in an hour, with his sight arti-ficially sharpened in the manner I have described, he would be able, in that brief time, to view scenes from the whole of human history as we know it, from the first man down to this very moment...

"And anyone will also concede that if such a traveller wished to observe this or that scene over a period, he would have to be flying at the same speed and in the same direction as light...

"Therefore, if we flew out of this room and continued flying at the speed of light, we would have constantly before us the selfsame image being presented to our gaze.

"However, if we suddenly found ourselves at something over three thousand two hundred and twenty five million miles from Earth and carried on flying at the speed of light, the Earth would appear before us as it had been twenty-four hours previously...

"And if we suddenly found ourselves three hundred and sixty-five times further than what I have just said, and still continued flying at the same speed, we would see things that had been played out on Earth a year previously...

"Then if we found ourselves another five, ten, a hundred or a thousand times further away than what I last said, and contin-ued flying at the speed of light, we could not fail to see what had happened on Earth five, ten, a hundred or a thousand years before that...

"Of course, our flight would have to be not perpendicular or random, but in the form of a huge cycloid so that our upward flight kept pace with the Earth's rotation about its axis, and also with the trajectory that it describes each year around the Sun.

"So not one of the scenes played out here on Earth has ceased to exist and they are all mirrored in the infinity of the cosmos.

"Therefore, an extraordinary speed will enable us to catch up with them and observe and investigate them to our heart's content.

"I have invented the means by which this journey of adventure can be realised, and though you will all be amazed at its unprecedented simplicity, it has proved its worth so often and so well that I am in the position today of being able to invite any of your august selves on the trip of a lifetime with me into the universe..."

The large room echoed to loud laughter, in part sceptical, in part derisive.

"Utopia! Pure hypothesis! Nonsense!" came from different quarters.

The laughter having largely subsided, the same grumpy voice that had interrupted my friend a short while before could be heard at the back:

"Jules Verne beat you to it: he took a similar trip to the Moon!"

Another hint of a smile flitted across my friend's face.

"I grant that you have a point there," he remarked, "but not the whole story. Because not even Jules Verne was the first to go on such an adventure. About twenty-five years before him, Edgar Allan Poe did something similar, and in the seventeenth century some fellow called Cyrano de Bergerac. The direction they took might have been the same, but the means and objectives differed... Those who undertook such trips in the past used complex means and their object was to amuse and instruct – while I employ the simplest means and my objective is..."

"To hell with objectives!" the grumpy voice in the middle chimed up a third time. "We want evidence that such an excursion really is possible!"

"You shall have the evidence forthwith," my friend replied. "I would ask each of you to write down on a small piece of paper the scene you would like to be seen anew..., then kindly delegate one member of your section to make the journey with me to conduct you."

So saying, my friend waved his hand several times and his instrument shot up into the air several times in a row, each time landing back on the table without a single sound.

These movements happened so fast that it was impossible to tell how many times it did happen. But it was proof that my friend's instrument really was something quite out of the ordinary.

After this preliminary demonstration there was a degree of commotion in the room. On slips of paper distributed by the staff, some of the guests were jotting down the scenes that they would like to be re-seen; others huddled in groups and were chatting, while my friend remained calmly at his table, waiting until everything was ready.

I, like all those present, might well have been convinced that the actual execution of a trip into the cosmos was unimaginable, yet I remained eager to see the manner of my friend's experiment.

I guessed, nay was practically certain, that it could not be done in any other way than as an optical illusion, so I was hugely curious to see how my friend was going to try to hoodwink such a large and select company.

His finesse as a magician had so far been genuinely

surprising, which is why I was so keen to see how he would execute his final demonstration and whether he would succeed in pulling the wool over my eyes too.

After the few minutes it took to write and collect the slips of paper, my friend took up his thread.

"Now please elect your delegate," he said. "The trip favours the brave – your delegate will stand with me inside the triangle and we will fly upwards…"

"Why elect? Can't we settle on volunteers instead?" the archbishop hazarded.

"All right, so who's going to volunteer?" my friend asked.

A deathly hush descended – no one came forward…

"So now's your best chance to apply your own faculties to whatever's coming next," I thought to myself, and when my friend repeated the question, I rose and made my way to his table.

I admit that I wasn't exactly at ease. The large company before which I was about to engage, jointly with my friend, in a spot of previously unimagined wizardry had stirred in my soul that mysterious, fear- and hope-filled tremor experienced by most people on making their first public appearance.

Seeing me come forward for the great adventure, he smiled his satisfaction and, once I reached his table, said:

"Sirs, the person who has come forward here is a friend of mine. Not wishing to be taken for a charlatan who only carries out his experiments with the collusion of those he trusts, I cannot accept his offer until you expressly and unequivocally declare that you accept him as your delegate."

The eyes of all were fixed on me in mute enquiry. It struck me that they were all seeking to detect from my features whether or not I deserved their trust.

After a pause, a voice from the throng did make itself heard:

"If there's no one else, what option do we have? But then, this is all about proof, so the person we delegate will have to prove to us the credibility of his report…"

"True! True!" came from several tables to the right.

"Agreed!" some said on the left.

"I am willing," I said somewhat diffidently, "not only to report faithfully on everything I see, but also – if possible – to provide evidence that it is true."

"So, permit me first and foremost," my friend began again, "to arrange in chronological order the slips of paper handed to me."

Then with remarkable speed he began so to order them.

Since I was standing right next to the table I was able to read quite clearly what was written on this slip or that.

In total, there were over four hundred of them, so, clearly, several guests had written more than one.

My friend was so deft at ordering the slips that he had it done in around five minutes.

"The first scene to be revisited according to these slips," he said, turning back to the guests, "occurred a hundred and nineteen days ago.

"So if we want to see it again, reflected within the infinity of the cosmos, we must first undertake the journey made by light in a hundred and nineteen days, and only then will we find ourselves at a spot from which to observe that scene – for a moment…

"If we wish to carry on observing it, we shall have to fly on at the speed of light.

"In that event, it will first be necessary to overtake time. Since light, as we know, travels over forty-two thousand miles in a second, it will cover two million five hundred and twenty thousand miles in a minute, a hundred and fifty-one million two hundred thousand miles in an hour, around three thousand six hundred and twenty-nine million miles in a single day, and in a hundred and nineteen days more than four hundred and thirty-one thousand eight hundred and fifty-one million miles.

"With the aid of my instrument we shall genuinely be that far from the Earth in the blink of an eye, after which we shall fly at the speed of light or slightly faster in a vast spiral corresponding to the Earth's rotation both round its own axis and round the Sun."

After this last account my friend shunted the table slightly forward and the triangle fell silently to the floor.

Thereupon he put on one of the pairs of peculiar spectacles and stepped into the triangle.

I followed his example, putting on the other pair of spectacles and entering the triangle by his side.

Silence reigned. No one stirred. All were visibly eager to see what would happen next.

It suddenly hit me that it surely wasn't possible for the instrument to breach the ceiling.

I looked up at the ceiling and saw a large circular opening, beyond which the sky was visible, along with some groups of stars.

However, before I could ask my friend about this odd change, which I hadn't registered before, I heard a clear tinkle like when someone taps a silver bell with a pebble, and we seemed at once to be flying upwards...

I say 'seemed' specifically, because the sight that had been there in the room a moment previously was still before my eyes, constant and motionless…

Before long, I asked my friend: "Are we flying, or not?" He was still holding the slips of paper written by the guests in one hand, and with the other he did seem to be steering the device.

"We are flying," came his reply. "Only at the speed of light for now, which is why you're still seeing what you saw before we took off. In a few seconds, I'll make an adjustment that will suddenly put us four hundred and thirty-one, eight hundred and fifty million miles from Earth, after which we'll fly on for a while at no more than the speed of light."

"All right," I said.

Shortly after, the scene floating before me seemed to be veiled in mist.

And before long, all I could see was a greyness turning slowly into darkness, until the dark before me seemed almost impenetrable.

"How come I can't see anything anymore?" I asked my friend.

"We're now as far from Earth," he said, "as light has travelled in a hundred and nineteen days. From a distance of four hundred and thirty-one thousand eight hundred and fifty-one million miles you are now seeing the landscape in which the scene of a hundred and nineteen days ago was played out at night. We're flying on at the speed of light. A slight touch of the main spring of my device will suffice for us to fly slightly faster and then the whole image will gradually open up before you."

I said nothing, for at that moment the darkness seemed to start turning grey, but this time with a hint of red.

S UDDENLY THE GREY GREW BRIGHTER and brighter and the image of a landscape seemed to step out of the mist before me. At first I could see only the vague outlines of mountains, forests, rivers, towns and villages. Here and there dark-red flames blazed...

But before long it all appeared in a brighter light. Now I could distinguish individual fields, roads, manors and cottages; I could also see entire villages in flames and that that entire landscape was ablaze will countless smaller fires, like fireflies...

The image slowly grew clearer.

I observed some odd shadows streaming in wild disarray not only along the roads, but also across fields and meadows...

Before long I could tell that these shadows were alive and consisted of countless atoms..., for I made them out to be cavalry and wagons and even infantry...

Here and there I could see smaller groups or tides fleeing in confusion, elsewhere condensed into seemingly motionless throngs...

I was still seeing it all in the half-light of a summer's night.

Gradually the image continued to clear... Close to villages in flames I saw a wild swirling... As if, here or there, crowds of people were going forward, elsewhere backwards.

Soon I could make out different groupings... By the light of smaller fires I saw small knots of people working hurriedly at something. Wagons and people were coming in haste to these various, and numerous, centres...

The strange image grew in plasticity... I could discern larger and smaller encampments of troops..., streams of people fleeing, and others pursuing them..., various groups where relief seemed to be being provided to the wounded...

Gradually I made out places literally peppered with fallen horses, overturned wagons and guns and people.

In such places there was a particular bustle... I could now distinguish individual people and saw some digging pits, others ferreting about and yet others collecting the fallen and carrying them off towards either the fires or the pits...

Within seconds I could tell that what I was seeing, having a bird's eye view of the landscape at eventide, was a battlefield after the fighting was done...

The image before me stretched far and wide for several miles. I could see almost a hundred settlements and towns, and thought I recognised some of the towns...

But the strange image was not static: the longer I looked, the clearer it became, while also changing...

I could see it all quite clearly, as if I were looking at a battle-field by daylight and from some high tower... Everything was alive, three-dimensional and full of colour, so I could have clearly made out every detail if I could just pay it the attention due...

But with the image constantly changing, I was taken by the whole and didn't have the time to observe and examine the details... For the same reason it is also impossible to describe the changing scene... It stretched away before my eyes like a panoramic view of a battle, but not from the start, as the battle begins, but from the end of the fighting gradually back to its beginning...

Thus I saw the image of people fleeing and in pursuit change gradually into one of people fighting, later preparing for battle and even later into one of two great armies getting ready to fight...

I saw an image of the desperate end of the fighting where the victory was decided, I saw an image of the fighting when victory leaned now one way, now the other...

Every detail was there to see: here a terrible bayonet attack by several regiments against the enemy's solid position, there a blood-bath of opposing cavalry regiments, there an artillery exchange supported by infantry fire and cavalry manoeuvring...

The overall physiognomy of the image kept changing: in places I could see nothing but thick white disks of smoke and here and there lightning flashes, evidence of the vicious exchange of fire between batteries... And then again I saw whole regiments of infantry and cavalry in battle formation, going hard at their desperate, bloody labours...

Thus did this horrific image roll out before me, very fast-moving, but perfectly clear...

And the whole overlain by a deathly silence. I couldn't hear the thunder of gunfire, the throbbing of the earth, the clatter of drums and the blare of trumpets, I couldn't hear the din and clatter of weapons, or the commands being given, the shouts and cries, or the wailing and groaning of the wounded...

All I could see was a living, horrendous, ever-changing image, but without the tumult and sounds and general din, like a grotesque pantomime of two vast, rabid hosts set on mutual extermination, all mirrored indelibly and eternally in the infinity of the universe...

And gradually the image of terrible, savage warfare changed into one progressively calmer, until I saw a perfectly calm, peaceful, enchanting landscape, shimmering in the golden glare of the summer sun...

And so amazing!

Surveying the whole image took so little time that I'd surveyed it quicker than the time it would take to read the description I've just given.

The optical illusion that my friend had treated me to with this first scene was a genuine surprise and most interesting. I now believed absolutely that his next demonstrations would be as successful as the first.

"I warrant I've just seen an image of the Battle of Sadowa," I remarked to my friend, who was standing silently next to me inside the triangle and calmly operating the strange device.

"You've guessed right," came the reply. "Now you'll see in rapid succession, though obviously in reverse order, all the battles of the Seven Days' War in Bohemia. To make it easy I'll assist you either with a brief commentary or a single word, so that you can watch at your ease, without having to ask things first."

"That suits me," I said and waited in silence for what was coming next.

I didn't have to wait long.

The image of a calm landscape began to grow dark, as if a veil of thick mist were being drawn across it, and seconds later I was looking at total darkness.

But hardly had I observed the change when the darkness began to yield to a mist and the mist to a clear half-light until once more a landscape shone in bright daylight and again I saw a battle...

The change I have just described was the same kind as we observe during experiments with so-called misty pictures, requiring the use of two cameras.

The image of the Battle of Sadowa changed into a peaceful landscape, this in turn into the Battle of Königinhof. Then came, in quick succession, the battles of Trautenau, Skalitz, Nachod, Gistchin, Münchengrätz and Podol interspersed with the numerous minor frays and skirmishes of the Austro-Prussian War.

"In those seven days," my friend noted, "no less than forty-five thousand people perished."

"Onward!" I called and in the twinkling of an eye the situation changed.

Again I saw images of war, this time from the Polish revolution and the First Schleswig War.

These were followed by the horrendous Battle of Puebla and scenes from the French invasion of Mexico, then the bloody Battle of Fredericksburg in America and a string of other battles great and small during the American Civil War.

"Wars in South America," my friend said, "cost five hundred and nineteen thousand lives, and the war in North America saw three hundred and eighty-one thousand victims."

"Onward!" I cried and at once witnessed the Day of Aspromonte, the conquest, and scenes from the Sicilian Revolution, the slaughter at Solferino, Magenta and a string of other battles great and small, then frightening and horrific scenes of revolution in India and no less bloody images of the Crimean War, from the terrible final attack on Sevastopol to the bloodshed of Balaclava and Inkerman.

"As many as seven hundred and eighty-five thousand people perished during the Crimean War," my friend remarked coldly.

"Onward!" I cried, and at once my eyes could feast on rapidly changing scenes from the street fighting during Napoleon's coup d'état, followed by an amazing medley of horrendously brutal scenes from the tumultuous years of 1849 and 1848, though consistently in reverse chronological order.

There were battlefields from almost the entire length and breadth of Europe.

I saw the encampment at Wilagosch, the Hungarians' defeats at Klein-Betschkerek, Szörög and Debreczin, the first Battle of Custoza, then the Battle of Segesvár between Hungarians and Russians, Görgei's defeats at Komárom and Szered, the bombardment of Pest, scenes from the June revolution in Paris, the seizure of Buda by the Hungarians, fighting on the barricades of Leipzig, the battles of Vácz, Nagy-Sarló, Gödöllö, Hatvan and Czegled, the siezure of Brescia by von Haynau, the battles at Novara and Mostar, scenes from the riots in Milan, the two-day Battle of Kápolna and the Battle of Szörik, where the Hungarians were defeated by Serbian General Knićanin.

I wanted to pass a comment, but my friend gestured for me to stay silent.

Next the Hungarian defeats at Belgrade and Trnava and the occupation of Raab by Windisch-Grätz, then scenes from the uprising in Lemberg, the defeat of the Hungarians at Schwechat, the storming and bombardment of Vienna, scenes from the October revolution in Vienna, from the troubles in Frankfurt and elsewhere, scenes from the June uprising in Prague and the bombardment of Prague by Windisch-Grätz, the battles of Vincenze, Curtatone and Santa Lucia, revolts in Dresden, Baden, Prussia and elsewhere, scenes from the

February uprising in Paris and the early turbulence brought about by the revolutionary movement in Italy.

"And can all the victims of these conflicts be calculated?" my friend asked, after the images had disappeared and before me briefly lay just quiet, enchanting landscapes.

"Onward!" I urged my friend and at once saw scenes from the Polish uprising of 1846 and after a pause various images from the republican disturbances in Paris, Toulon and Grenoble in 1843, the capture of Warsaw by Russian troops in 1831, riots in Dresden and the Battle of Ostrolenka.

I stared briefly at this ghastly fratricidal conflict, then asked: "How far are we from Earth?"

"About forty-six billion miles," he replied.

Then I saw images from the July revolution in Paris, the capture of Erivan Fortress by Paskevich and the bloody Battle of Missolonghi, followed in turn by various scenes from the independence struggles on the Iberian Peninsular and in Greece.

After a longer interval I again saw a horrific, great battle.

"How far are we from Earth?" I asked.

"About sixty-eight billion miles," my friend replied. "Right now you're observing the Battle of Waterloo."

As my friend continued with his brief account I saw in rapid succession the slaughter of Leipzig, which went on for three days, the battles at Montmartre outside Paris, by Kulm in Bohemia and at Bautzen, then the passage of the remnant of the French army through Berezino, the Battle of Jarosławiec, the Fire of Moscow and the Battle of Borodino; then the bloody Battle of Wagram and the indecisive Battle of Aspern-Essling; a string of images of the revolutions in Peru and Mexico and the Spanish wars, then more battles during the Napoleonic Wars: Eylau, Jena and Auerstädt, the murderous Battle of Austerlitz and the terrifyingly beautiful, naval Battle of Trafalgar.

I stared into my friend's face, then immediately returned my gaze to the spot where I'd seen those images of warfare.

Next came scenes from the uprising of the Serbs under 'Black George', horrific images of the unrest on Santo Domingo and in Switzerland, and yet more from the Napoleonic wars: the battles of Hohenlinden and Marengo, the land Battle of Abukir, at which Napoleon beat the Turks, and the naval battle near the same town, when the French navy was destroyed by Nelson; then various battles large and small in Egypt, right back to the Battle of the Pyramids.

Meanwhile there was the fighting in Holland and Switzerland, the crushing of Venice and the battles at La Favorita, Rivoli, Arcole and Lodi...

"Is it possible to calculate the numbers of human lives lost to the account of the ambition of a single despot, Napoleon?" my friend mused.

I didn't reply.

We flew a little further back in time.

I saw the terrible fighting that preceded the capture of Praga by Suvorov, the fratricidal Battle of Maciejowice, where Kościuszko, having been defeated by Suvorov, fell injured to the ground with a cry of 'Finis Poloniae', and the capture of Wilno by the Russian army.

Next came horrendous images from the French Revolution, the Kościuszko Uprising in Warsaw and the revolt in Cracow, then a string of bloody wars with the Turks, the independence struggle in North America, in which Washington and Franklin played the most important roles; then scenes from the Seven Years' War, especially the battles near Neu-Kolin and Prague, then the conquest of Prague by the combined forces of Bavaria, Saxony and France, scenes from the 1740 War of the Austrian Succession; the 1709 Battle of Poltava and many other images from the brutal Great Northern War between Russians and Swedes, the Battle of Narva, then scenes from the War of the Spanish Succession, and in turn Sobieski's defeat of the Turks at Vienna and the French war with the Spaniards and Dutch.

Then I saw the brutal Battle of Polonka in 1660, where the Russians were defeated by Sapieha and Czarniecki, the three-day Battle of Praga and the capture of Warsaw by Karl Gustav, the defeat of the Poles under Batow by Bohdan Khmelnicky's army.

I wanted to ask how far we from Earth now, but the images were hurtling past so fast that they held my attention to the exclusion of all else.

I saw the 1650 Battle of Dunbar, where Cromwell was triumphant, then lots more battles right back to 1644 and Marston Moor, where ten thousand Royalists fell.

And interspersed between them were scenes from the Swedish campaign in Bohemia: the defence of the Old Town bridge towers and the capture of Malá Strana and Hradčany.

Next came some brutal scenes from the Thirty Years' War: amongst others I saw the 1632 Battle of Lützen, the destruction of Magdeburg, and the campaigns and battles in which Wallenstein and Tilly played the leading roles; then the execution of Bohemian patriots on the Old Town Square and eventually the Battle of the White Mountain.

I looked long at this image of the Bohemians' defeat...

"And how far are we from Earth now?" I asked my friend.

"Around three hundred and twenty-five billion miles," he replied, adding: "But onwards! Time is short..."

And instantly we flew on.

I saw many more terrible, bloody scenes: the slaughtering of the Huguenots, scenes from the religious wars in France, from the wars in which the Duke of Alba played the main part, from the peasant wars etc. These were followed by scenes of mass murder in Peru, Mexico and other countries in Latin America, where the greed of Europeans brought ruination.

"Onward! Onward!" I cried in my impatience.

After a short interval I saw the defeats of Matthias Corvinus, the Novgorodians, the Tatars outside Moscow and of the fanatical German, anti-Hussite crusaders at Nýrsko in 1431.

There was the capture of Sion Castle in 1437 and the fratricidal Battle of Lipany, the terrible defeat of the Germans at Domažlice and, in between, various scenes from Joan of Arc's fight against the English, then the Bohemians' capture of Lubno in Upper Lusatia, the bloody Battle of Světlá, where Albrecht's troops were thrashed by the Taborites and the radical Hussite Orphans' Union; the Battle of Aussig, where Prokop Holý and twenty thousand men defeated seventy thousand Germans; Žižka's camp and Žižka himself dying at Přibyslav.

My soul was briefly overcome with sorrow, though my attention was instantly grabbed by the succession of bloody Hussite battles under Žižka's leadership, notably at Česká Skalice and Jaroměř, the defeat of the Praguers at Strachov, the Battle of Hořice, the defeat of Zikmund's hosts at Německý Brod, the slaughter of the Adamites on an island in the Nežárka, the defeat of the crusaders at Saaz, the defeat of the aristocrats at Malešov, the capture of Prague Castle, Jaroměř, Litomyšl and Beroun; then the defeat of Zikmund's army beneath Vyšehrad, of the Catholic lords at Bor near Horažďovice, of Zikmund's crusaders between Žižkov and Hradčany, and the Battle of Sudoměř.

After another short pause I also saw the terrible scene of John Huss being burned at the stake in Constance.

Quite literally, all these images flew past my eyes – I could barely keep up with them, barely keep up with my friend's commentary.

The blood had started to run to my head and I began to feel slightly giddy.

"How far are we now?" I asked.

"Roughly five hundred and ninety-eight billion miles," my friend replied calmly. "We've only flown through a period of about four hundred and fifty-one years, so we still have about ten times as far to go before we reach the point from which we can observe scenes from the time of the first humans... We still need to fly a trivial distance – about six thousand billion miles, that is, to reach the sphere of magnitude 12 stars, whose light takes over four thousand years to reach Earth... Look! How easy it is to say! And yet every second we cover more than forty-two thousand miles, but without overtaking light..."

"And is it possible to cover the distance in any short interval of our choosing?" I asked, and it never occurred to me that I couldn't even imagine such a phenomenal distance.

"Of course," my friend replied.

"But tell me, just what is this astonishing engine that powers our device at such a speed through the cosmos?"

"Later, later!" he replied. "I have to keep steering... One tiny mistake and we'd lose our equilibrium and go hurtling downwards..."

"Where to?" I asked.

"How am I supposed to know?"

"So onward! But fast!" I spurred him on.

"If we want to get the trip over and done with inside an hour, we'll have to confine ourselves from now on to just a few of the most important scenes."

"But fast, fast!" I persisted.

And in no time I was again seeing an amazing, fearsome panorama of battles...

The images followed one another at a staggering speed, though each could be made out quite clearly.

And wondrous to relate!

This time the images of battles and skirmishes were mingled with scenes of a different kind, but in them all there was still fighting...

Thus did another hundred or so images pass before my eyes along with various scenes in which the animality of human nature was triumphant, where brute force or guile and skulduggery prevailed over weakness and innocence...

Suddenly I noticed that at one change of scene the dark was there too long.

"What's that?" I asked in my impatience.

"I'm steering it for you be able to catch the last scene... We're far higher than the stars of magnitude 12, in spheres from which light travels to Earth over a period of some six thousand years...

"Anyway, this time we're going to change the way we look on. When we reach the point from which the scene can be observed, I'll stop the appliance and let it just rotate appropriately, commensurate to the rotation of the Earth about its axis and around the sun, so that the image will open out before your eyes in its natural chronological progression, and not in reverse chronology as it has been till now."

Before long I was watching as a number of brighter rays shoot out from the pitch black into which I'd been staring.

The dark began to change into a grey mist, which then suddenly dispersed. Emerging from the mist I saw the dark contours of a wild barren landscape, which grew ever more clearly defined.

Before long the image before me was quite clear.

I could see a bare, rocky plain ending in a dense forest of fir, above that, rising towards a cloudy sky, the dark outline of a high mountain range.

Spread over the landscape was an inhospitable, stifling greyness, like before a storm, and just now and then a glint of sunlight flashed between the heavy clouds, allowing the landscape to shine ever so briefly in a golden radiance...

Shortly I was able to distinguish smaller objects. Hard by the forest next to a kind of lair I made out a group of people – a young woman and three children... Two of the children are clinging fearfully to their mother, while the third, a baby, which the mother is holding in her arms, is looking into its mother's eyes with a blissful smile on its innocent little face...

The mother's pale features display, however, fear and unutterable horror.

Her eyes are fixed on the dark forest undergrowth, her naked, buxom body is shaking, and as she clutches her naked infant to her breasts with her left hand, she reaches for the other two naked children with her right hand as if wanting to protect them as they huddle up to her in fear.

At that instant, a little further off, a slim young man shoots out of the forest, carrying his prey, a female deer, across his shoulders.

His face speaks not of fear, but of concern...

He is followed at speed out of the forest by another man of an athletic build. His cloddish face is ablaze with bestial rage...

Both are naked...

Having dropped the deer, the first one stands to face the second, determined to put up a fight, though the second had come charging after him brandishing a club with his muscular right arm.

The battle commences... From a distance, the woman watches on in mortal distress... It is a brutal, ferocious fight to the death... But it only takes seconds...

The first man sinks to the ground – the athlete has smashed his skull open...

The face of the woman, who has watched the ghastly fight in anguish, reveals her despair... Clasping the baby even more firmly to her wildly heaving bosom, she flees..., the other two children follow her..., until they vanish in the gloom of the forest...

I watched the image, bereft of words, as it began to be veiled in mist...

I still caught sight of the athletic second man hauling his booty, the deer, paid for by the death of another man, off into the forest... Then a dense, total darkness cloaked the terrible scene completely...

I was overcome with anguish.

I could feel the blood coursing intemperately through my veins, driving up towards my brain, and began feeling dizzy.

I wanted to say something to my friend, but the words got clogged in my throat. My friend was the first to speak.

"You've just seen the first fight of the first people... We've reached our destination... And all you have seen from start to finish has been constant strife, the mutual elimination and butchery of the most perfect of God's creatures...

"This battle has been raging since the start of time...

"And over the course of a few thousand years mankind has sought to lay down the main principle of life, kidding itself that the world is governed by the principle of love and humanity... And it has taken millennia for mankind to recognise at last that it has been mistaken, deluded...

"After thousands of years it has come to recognise just how merciless and terrible is the god who has doomed to destruction all that he has made weaker and more powerless; after thousands of years man now recognises that life is nothing but an eternal fight for survival...

"And how has mankind responded to this terrible god?...

"Some have sought power and glory, others have hankered after wealth, while yet others have pampered their petty psyches in the sweet embrace of sentimentality – whereas the cold intellect of Newton, which had seen through the pettiness and perversion of all human strivings, struck nothing but horror and awe in everyone...

"They have been terrified by the cold, but honest numbers by which the universe has been measured, horrified at the inexorable rigour of his ice-cold, but incontrovertible calculations – and lo and behold! – humanity now stands before the throne of the Darwinian god, a hideous, merciless god of might and main...

"For years this god has been harried by certain elements, but the goal of their feeble fight is for the throne of the god of might and main to be re-occupied by the deposed, murky god of religious fanaticism...

"But the fight against the Darwinian god is an uneven fight. You won't depose him even if this great feat of arms were taken up by the entire world... The only way to undermine this god's throne is by the principles of humanism..."

My friend lapsed into silence.

His words rang like thunder, like when a severe, scrupulous judge issues an angry rebuke...

However, I couldn't make out his face, because we were in utter, impenetrable darkness. I said nothing...

Then suddenly he spoke again:

"What's this? Our appliance has developed a wobble... We seem to have lost equilibrium... We're dropping!..."

My friend's voice sounded so perturbed that my heart turned to ice. My disquiet instantly changed into unutterable anguish...

"Let go!" my friend screamed. "One of us has to be sacrificed!... Or we'll both perish!..."

I didn't respond; I couldn't have responded. All I could feel was my senses abandoning me.

"Let go! Or I'll knock you down!" he implored me again.

"At least tell me what your device is called!" I managed to blurt out.

Then I felt the contrivance overturn... We were flying headlong downwards...

I let go...

I thought I heard my friend's wild laughter and the words:

"Farewell forever!... My device is familiar to the entire world... For it is that which eternally brings things to life, is eternally creative – imagination..."

My friend's voice had a dull ring to it; I could barely catch the last words... I completely lost consciousness.

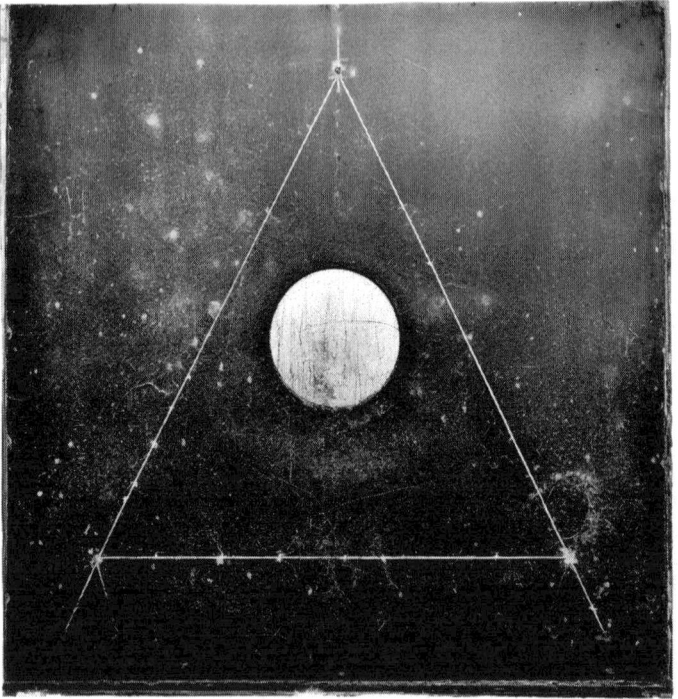

ANYONE WHO HAS EVER FALLEN ASLEEP, in the autumn, beside an open window, and has then suddenly come to, knows the peculiar frosty sensation that accompanies the awakening...

A similar chill now shot through my body as, coming out of my semi-conscious dream, I noticed that the ochrous half-light of dawn was coming in through the half-open window of my lonely garret...

I looked about me in bewilderment and my first thought honed itself involuntarily into a question:

"Was that real, a chimaera or a dream?"

But my senses were so dulled that I couldn't pinpoint the answer.

All I can remember is the immediate realisation that Dr Sperlich, who had confirmed, in the summer house of the Princes Kinsky, that my friend was dead, had himself died several years previously, and that in the house itself there had never been, nor were there now, any corridors such as I had been wandering up and down, lost...

I also recall that I'd been sitting at my desk with a book on astronomy open before me, which I'd apparently been reading before nodding off...

More than that I don't remember. My soul began to faint away again...

After a time I came round...

I was lying on my bed and next to the bed my dear old mother was kneeling... I opened my eyes wide and gazed into her honest, wrinkled face and my soul felt a tremor of unutterable bliss...

"Ah, my child, my child, what has been happening to you?" I heard her say. "They came running to fetch me, saying you were unconscious – and for three days by then..."

"Three days?" was my immediate response.

"Three – ," my mother repeated. "The doctor's been coming in several times a day and advises nothing but peace and quiet... He said something vague about signs of... lunacy..."

A gleam of clarity flared up through my gloomy soul. I shivered...

"And he said you should give up your studies for a while..."

My mother rose to her feet, bent down over me and kissed me gently on the brow – – –

I FOLLOWED THE DOCTOR'S ADVICE...

I temporarily gave up my studies, though the thoughts that had pursued me back then keep coming back to me even after all these years...

A postscript on the toponymy
of *Newton's Brain*
by David Short

Much of the 'action' of this *romanet[t]o* – a Poe-esque 'tale of mystery', a genre first employed in Czech by Jakub Arbes (1840–1914), though given its cod-Italian name *romaneto* by Jan Neruda (1834–91) – takes place during the Austro-Prussian War, or Seven Weeks' War, of 1866. The translator recalls from his school days in the 1950s one major battle in that encounter, to wit the Battle of Sadowa. Generally, English historians writing of this war have used the German names of the places involved (hence *Sadowa*), since these would have taken precedence, under the old Austrian Empire, over names in the local vernaculars. For this reason, as befitting the historical context and the language of the translation, I have germanised all the names of places on Czech soil (Eastern Bohemia) where battles in that war were fought. Below is a glossary of those mentioned, giving the names that will be encountered by today's travellers or on Czech maps (or by the reader of Arbes's original text):

Gitschin	Jičín
Königgrätz	Hradec Králové, archaically Králové Hradec
Königinhof	Dvůr Králové, archaically Králové Dvůr
Münchengrätz	Mnichovo Hradiště
Nachod	Náchod
Nechanitz	Nechanice
Neu-Kolin	Kolín
Podol	Podolí

Problus	Probluz
Sadowa	Sadová
Skalitz	Česká Skalice
Smirschitz	Smiřice
Trautenau	Trutnov

The war in question took place between the 7th or 17th June (depending on what action on the part of the Prussians is taken as the start) and 23rd of August 1866, when the peace agreement was signed. The battles mentioned in the book took place at: Sadowa on 3rd July; Königinhof on 29th June; Trautenau on 27th-28th June; Skalitz on 28th June; Nachod on 27th June; Gitschin on 29th June; Münchengrätz on 28th June; and Podol on 26th-27th June. (The Battle of Hühnerwasser [Kuřivody, 26th June] has not, apparently, merited a mention.) It follows that Arbes's hero's instrument got the chronology slightly confused! The earlier reference in the text to the 'Seven Days' War' is also unusual: the Austro-Prussian War proper is usually referred to alternatively as the Seven *Weeks* War, when not labelled the 'German War' or the 'War of German on German', though the period when these battles took place on the soil of Eastern Bohemia is indeed spread over just 7–8 days. (NB: There *is* a Seven Days' War in Czech history [1919], but with Poland and after Arbes had died [1914].) Note also the reference to the Battle of Kulm, where Arbes himself gives the German name instead of Cz. *Chlumec* (1813, during the War of the Sixth Coalition – a defeat for Napoleon in northern Bohemia, following his victory at Dresden).

Places affected by the First Italian War of Independence (also 1848–49) or the Russo-Persian War (1826–28), amongst others witnessed by the travellers, require no further commentary and can be easily identified by atlas or encyclopaedia. And places touched on in connection with the Hussite Wars do not generally create any German-Czech confusion, unlike the Austro-Prussian War above. However, when it comes to the Polish-Russian War or November Uprising (1830–31), the Hungarian Revolution and the Serb Uprising (both 1848–49), I believe the following place-names involved do merit clarification:

Czegled, old spelling of *Cegléd*: Ger. *Zieglet*, a city in Pest County, Budapest Metropolitan Area, Hungary, approximately 70 km (43 m.) southeast of Budapest.

Debreczin: Hun. *Debrecen*, Ger. *Debrezin*, a major city of Hungary.

Gödöllő: Ger. *Getterle*; Slk.: *Jedľovo*), a town in Pest County, Hungary, c. 30 km (20 m.) northeast from the outskirts of Budapest.

Hatvan is a town in Heves County, Hungary, *c.* 50 km (31 m.) NE of Budapest. *Hatvan* is the Hungarian word for 'sixty'.

Klein-Betschkerek: Rom. *Becicherecu-Mic* (also Hun. *Kisbecskerek*; Srb. *Mali Bečkerek*), a commune in Timiş County, in the Romanian Banat.

Komárom: Slk. *Komárno*, a small town still divided between Hungary and Slovakia.

Lemberg: today's *Lviv* (Ukr.), long known as Rus. *Lvov* or Pol. *Lwów*, the largest city in western Ukraine, at the time in Austrian Galicia, and heavily Germanised.

Nagy-Sarló = Nagy-Salló: Slk. *Veľké Šarluchy*, today renamed as *Tekovské Lužany*, Slovakia.

Ostrolenka: Pol. *Ostrołęka*, where the battle of 26 May 1831 was one
of the largest engagements of Poland's November Uprising.
Raab (Ger.) = Hun. *Györ*, Cz. *Ráb*: the most important city of
northwest Hungary, halfway between Budapest and Vienna.
Segesvár: now *Sighişoara*, Romania.
Szered: Sereď in Slovakia.
Szörög: Szőreg (Serb. *Cupuz, Sirig*) is a village, since 1973 part of
the city of Szeged in Czongrád County (in the former Banat,
and the site of a battle which the Hungarians lost). At a
later point in the story there is a reference to another place,
Szörik, which may or may not be thought of as the same,
but appearing as another Hungarian loss to the Serbian
voivode Knićanin. It has not been possible to ascertain what
battle this was, or where 'Szörik' is. Knićanin certainly did
defeat the Hungarians at least twice.
Vácz, today spelled *Vác*: Slk. *Vacov,* Ger. *Waitzen*, between
Budapest and the Slovak frontier.
Kápolna: a village in Heves County, Hungary, battle fought here
on 26–27 Feb. 1849.
Wilagosch: Hung. *Világos*, now Şiria, Romania.

In the translation, the name of Prague is duly given in its English
form, and the name of Königsberg is retained, as Arbes has it
anyway, in German. It does have a Czech name, Královec, but
since it lies/lay in East Prussia, this would have been inappropri-
ate. However, the king (*König, král*) after whom it is named was
Ottakar II of Bohemia; Arbes clearly liked his contexts to have a
Czech dimension (cf. Marston Moor below). Today we all know
the city as Kaliningrad in the Soviet/Russian exclave on the Baltic
Sea, between Lithuania and Poland.

As for the two British place names occurring the text, both Dunbar and Marston Moor are misspelt, as *Dumbar*[20] and *Marstonmoor*, respectively. There could, in the spirit of the friends' journey back through time, have been glimpses of countless other bloodbaths on English or Scottish soil. However, Arbes's original Czech readership may have been more aware of battles during the English Civil War than of others on this side of the Channel, not least because the Royalists were commanded at Marston Moor by the Prague-born Prince Rupert of the Rhine, son of Frederick V, Elector Palatine and King of Bohemia (and Duke of Cumberland), and his wife Elizabeth, the eldest daughter of James VI of Scotland and I of England, known as 'The Winter Queen'.[21] According to Wikipedia, Cromwell's side lost a mere 300 men, Prince Rupert lost 4,000 killed and 1,500 captured. Any affinity of Arbes and the Czechs to this event may account for the discrepancy between the numbers lost on the Royalist side in the story (10,000) and in Wikipedia.[22]

It should not be forgotten that Rupert was also a founding member of the Royal Society, even converting some rooms

20 Easily explained as reflecting the unconscious assimilation of dental nasal [n] to dental labial [m] before labial [b], as can be heard, if closely observed, in pronunciations of, say, *gunboat* as 'gumboat'.

21 She is the person behind English pubs called *The Queen of Bohemia*, now all [?] defunct or renamed, the last [?], in Hampstead, quite recently

22 Merely as an aside: among the defeated Royalist commanders at Marston Moor was William Cavendish, Duke of Newcastle (1593-1676), who, after fleeing the country and taking refuge in Paris in 1645, married Margaret Lucas, a maid of honour to Queen Henrietta Maria. She is the memorably outrageous, early outspoken feminist and prolific pen-woman Margaret (Mad Madge) Cavendish (1623-73), whose published works included The Blazing World, variously described as an early or the earliest work of science fiction in English literature involving travel to a fantastical other world, or at least as a forerunner of science fiction.

at Windsor Castle into a serious laboratory. He is credited with numerous inventions, many of them military, and with defining, though not solving, the paradox known as Prince Rupert's *Cube*. In many respects, he was a worthy (incidental?) forerunner of Arbes's narrator's friend, who is only once identified by name – as Bedřich Wünscher. It may, or may not, be entirely coincidental that Rupert's begetter was a Frederick and that the begetter of the 'invention' in the story (also geometrical, involving a *triangle*) is called Bedřich (Czech for Frederick) – with, moreover, the 'aspirational' and German surname of Wünscher, i.e. 'he who wishes'.

As a matter of interest, Prince Rupert is remembered through the length and breadth of England in street names: there are (at the time of writing) two instances of Prince Rupert Avenue,[23] two of Prince Rupert Way[24] and four of Prince Rupert Road.[25] And there is a Prince Rupert pub and Prince Rupert Hotel. [26] Additionally there are 24 instances of Rupert Street (including one in Scotland, plus one in London that has been renamed),[27] two of Rupert Square,[28] 15 of Rupert

---

23 In Desborough (Kettering) and Powick (Worcester).

24 In Heathfield (Newton Abbot) and Norwich.

25 In Ledbury, London SE9, Stourport-on-Severn and Worcester.

26 In Newark-on-Trent and Shrewsbury respectively.

27 In Biddulph, Bolton, Bristol BS1, Bristol BS5 (Barton Hill), Carnforth, Chesterfield (Waterloo), Glasgow G4, Ilkestone, Keighley BD21, Keighley BD22 (Cross Roads), Leicester, London W1, Manchester (Newton Heath), Manchester (Radcliffe), Nelson, Norwich, Reading, Rochdale, Stockport, Stockton-on-Tees, Sunderland, Taunton, Wigan, Wolverhampton, and the former Rupert St., now Goodman St., London E1.

28 In Reading (with Rupert Walk and Cumberland Rd. nearby, remembering the Siege of Reading, 1642–43) and Sunderland.

Road,[29] two of Rupert Avenue[30] and one Rupert Way,[31] any or all of which *may* be in memory of the same Prince. And in addition to that there are – some *possibly* in memory of the Prince's father, Frederick the Elector Palatine and Winter King – four cases of Palatine Avenue,[32] ten of Palatine Road,[33] five of Palatine Street[34] two of Palatine Square[35] and one of Palatine Place.[36] And at least four pubs/hotels called The Palatine.[37] And there's the Palatine Centre at Durham University. All that is to say nothing of what Frederick may lie behind the numerous Frederick Streets and so on in England. Clearly a lot of work in scores of local archives would be necessary to clinch this question.

---

29 In Bingham (Nottingham), Chaddesden (Derby), Coventry, Grimsby, Guildford, Ilkley, Liverpool (Huyton), London N19 (Upper Holloway), London NW6 (Kilburn), London W4 (Chiswick), Market Harborough, Newbury, Oxford (Cowley), Sheffield and Southminster.

30 In High Wycombe and Wembley

31 In Thame.

32 In Lancaster, London N16, Manchester M20 and Rochdale.

33 In Blackburn, Blackpool, Bromborough, Goring-by-Sea, London N16, Manchester M20/22, Rochdale, Southport (Birkdale), Thornton-Cleveleys and Wallasey

34 In Bolton, Manchester (Denton), Nottingham, Ramsbottom and Rochdale

35 In Burnley and Leigh

36 In Gateshead

37 In Hadfield, Liverpool (Garston), Morecambe and Salford.

FORTHCOMING TITLES

Jantar is an independent publisher based in London that has been praised widely for its choice of texts, artwork, editorial rigour and use of very rare and sometimes unique fonts in all its books. Jantar's guiding principle is to select, publish and make accessible previously inaccessible works of Central European literary fiction through translations into English… texts 'trapped in amber'.

Since its foundation in 2011, Jantar's list has been made up, mostly, of works of literary fiction. In 2023, we begin to broaden our mission to include works of science fiction from Central Europe, a region rich in authors and stories in this genre.

Being Jantar, we begin our new SF list with the first recognised works in the genre written in Czech and Slovak. *Newton's Brain* by Jakub Arbes and published in a new translation by David Short, was first published in 1877, 18 years before *The Time Machine* by H.G. Wells. It first appeared in English translation in 1892. Arbes was much admired by Émile Zola.

Our second SF title was written in an uncodified version of 'Old Slovak' and published in 1856. *The Science of the Stars* by Gustáv Reuss is arguably the first title to feature a balloon travelling to the moon. It is certainly the first to appear in any version of the Slovak language.

Also forthcoming in 2024, is a new novella by Balla, *Among the Ruins*, and our first novels translated from German. In May, we shall publish *Winterberg's Last Journey* by Jaroslav Rudiš. Later in the year, we launch the much-anticipated new translation of *The Grandmother* by Božena Němcová. Together with Erben's *Kytice* (Jantar 2014) and Mácha's *May* (Jantar 2025), *The Grandmother* is one of the three founding works of modern Czech Literature. This new and complete translation will show, for the first time to English-language readers, the subversive, feminist, anti-theological and anti-Habsburg elements in this classic text. It will be published in a regular prose version and another illustrated by Míla Fürstová.

These titles and all our other titles can be purchased postage-free world-wide from our website:
www.JantarPublishing.com

SELECTED TITLES PUBLISHED BY JANTAR

Barcode is one of many collections of short stories published by Jantar in English. In 2022, we published **DEAD** and ***Mothers and Truckers*** by Balla and Ivana Dobrakovová respectively. Another, very popular, collection of short stories was published in 2018 called **And My Head Exploded**. Featuring 10 short stories, the book features works and authors from the Bohemian fin-de-siècle era never previously translated into English.

In 2017, we published ***Fox Season*** by Agnieszka Dale, a collection of dazzling stories set in a London bracing itself for Brexit. It is now making its first appearance on university literature courses. The stories were described by Zoë Apostolides in the *Financial Times* as 'fascinating and refreshingly honest stares at life in a foreign place, whatever that definition might be'.

City of Torment by Daniela Hodrová, published in 2021 attracted very positive reviews in *The Los Angeles Review of Books*, *The Irish Times* and *New European Review*. The book begins, 'Alice Davidovič would have never thought the window of her childhood room hung so low above the Olšany cemetery that a body could travel the distance in less than two seconds.'

Birds of Verhovina by Ádám Bodor contains a cast of weirdos and miscreants left to make their own way in the Carpathian Mountains. It was described by Diána Vonnák in *The Times Literary Supplement* as 'one of those places you might visit but might never leave; it is reality on its way to becoming allegory'.

Carbide by Andriy Lyubka was published at the end of 2020 when we all thought the worst that could happen was to be locked-down by a global pandemic. Set in what now appears to be the very quaint Ukraine prior to its attempted evisceration by Russia, Lyubka describes another Carpathian periphery world populated by criminals, corrupt local officials and a delusional history teacher. *Carbide* was described by Kate Tsurkan in *The Los Angeles Review of Books* as 'a fast-paced tragicomedy which establishes the young author as Ukraine's modern-day Voltaire'.

These titles and all our other titles can be purchased postage-free world-wide from our website:
www.JantarPublishing.com